The Case of the Missing Stradivarius

Emanuel E. Garcia

First published in 2009 by
The Irregular Special Press,
for Baker Street Studios Ltd,
Endeavour House,
170 Woodland Road, Sawston,
Cambridge, CB22 3DX, UK.

ISBN: 1-901091-36-8 (10 digit)
ISBN: 978-1-901091-36-6 (13 digit)

Cover Concept: Antony J. Richards.

Back Cover Illustration: Inside the Langham Hotel from an original watercolour by
Nikki Sims.

Typeset in 8/11/20pt Palatino

Contents

Foreword

The violin, of all musical instruments, has exerted the greatest fascination on the imagination and inspired the profoundest reverence. It appeared relatively suddenly in the mid-16th century in Cremona, Italy, the handiwork of Andrea Amati (and perhaps a few others), who seemed rather miraculously to have arrived at the ideal shape for the creation and projection of the most pleasing and exciting musical sonorities, upon which no-one has since been able to improve.

Mystery and controversy engulf virtually everything about it – its evolution and origins, its construction, its acoustical properties, its architectural design, its physics, its allure as a work of art, and even its uncanny and inimitable power to move the soul. What is *not* controversial is the incomparability of the sound of a Stradivarius violin in the hands of true virtuoso, eliciting with its warmth, brilliance and carrying power an unrivalled depth and palette of emotion. The tradition of violin-making established by Amati found its culmination in that very same Cremona during the late 17th and early 18th centuries, where a group of artisans, chief among whom was Antonio Stradivari, produced instruments that have been and still are the prized possessions of the world's greatest violinists.

The violins of Stradivari have been meticulously copied, measured and subjected to extensive scientific analysis. Many theories have been propounded to account for their uniqueness, including the climatic (cold weather promoting the growth of denser and hence more uniformly resonant wood), the physical (the specific shape and contours of the body of the instrument, in addition to wood type), the chemical (Stradivari's secret varnish), the artistic (Stradivari's genius in craftsmanship), and even the biological (fungal action).

Modern luthiers, despite far greater knowledge of acoustics and musical science, have yet to equal the qualities possessed by the stringed instruments of Stradivari. Or have they? Debates about their relative merits continue, and blind listening tests have thrown doubt on the so-called magical properties of the master's violins. But for all this, Stradivari's instruments – or occasionally those of his Cremonese rival Giuseppe Guarneri – are the first choice of virtually every preeminent soloist today.

Aside from the legacy of his instruments, relatively little is known about the facts of Antonio Stradivari's life. He was undoubtedly born in Cremona, but we are not sure exactly when (we believe 1644 to be the year of his birth). He is thought to have been apprenticed to Nicolò Amati (grandson of Andrea), but even this assumption has been challenged. What we do know is that when he eventually established his own workshop in the Piazza San Domenico, he proved to be a restless and enterprising craftsman. By the late 1680s he was producing instruments of remarkable aesthetic beauty, and royal commissions were coming his way – from James II of England, and Cosimo de' Medici of Tuscany, for example. He experimented tirelessly with many aspects of the violin in his earlier years, including the manufacture of a long-pattern fiddle, before settling on a form to which he would adhere until his death in 1737 (at the advanced age of ninety-four!), though not without experimenting continuously in smaller ways. His so-called 'golden period' – from 1700 until approximately 1720 – was marked by personal affluence and the consistent production of violins of the highest quality, made from superb woods sculpted with exquisite craftsmanship. These can be heard in concert halls around the world today.

All told Stradivari made over a thousand instruments (violins, cellos, violas and guitars), six hundred of which are known to have survived. A genuine Stradivarius violin of superior quality is priceless, and is regarded by the expert player who is fortunate enough to own it not as an object but as an animate and irreplaceable being.

The construction of a decent violin is no easy feat. The selection of wood and the testing of its resonances, the carving of the sound-holes, the curving of the bouts, the arching of the back and the belly, the calibration of the thicknesses of the body, the proper application of varnish, the laying in of the purfling – all of these tasks demand patience, judgment, craft and artistry.

But if making a violin is difficult, how then can one describe the actual playing of it? Merely sounding a passable note on a violin is regarded as a marvel. Years of disciplined practice beginning in toddlerhood, combined with innate musical sense, the exposure to superb teachers and magnificent compositions: all of these might be present but not a fine violinist make!

Here lies yet another and even more important mystery: that of the great performing musician.

Technical ability – though of extraordinary importance – does not alone explain why some virtuosi achieve true artistic greatness, and others do not. A brief glance at the pantheon of musical giants – violinists such as Joachim, Enescu, Francescatti, Thibaud, Grumiaux, Szigeti, Milstein, Elman, Kreisler, Oistrakh, Heifetz, Menuhin and many others – reveals players of varying personalities, musical upbringing and practice habits, and widely diverging approaches to performance and musical interpretation.

No instrument, however, is more demanding than the violin – nor more susceptible to the slightest vagaries of touch. Playing consistently in tune constitutes an enormous and never-ending challenge to the player. And beyond matters of technique lie those of interpretation: How does the violinist express most fully the beauties of the Beethoven concerto or a Bach partita? What allows him or her to create music that is alive and moving to an audience? How critical – how emotional! – is the relationship of the violinist to the violin itself? How does the artistic temperament affect those within its orb? What in fact is the interpretation of a musical score all about?

This work of fiction is an attempt to engage the reader in contemplating such mysteries, albeit principally through an imagined character, one Signor Donato del Nero. In del Nero, as in his real-life predecessors – Tartini, Viotti, Lipinsky, Paganini, Vieuxtemps, Kreutzer, Wieniawski, Ysaÿe, Bull, Sarasate, Joachim and others – reside the ambiguities, drive, eccentricities and immense talent of a supreme virtuoso of the violin – and in his approach to music, perhaps something more.

Naturally any conjunction of fiction and mystery cannot help but bring to mind the figure of Mr Sherlock Holmes, arguably the most recognisable name in all of literature. Indeed, so remarkable is his character that he has been mistaken by many for a living breathing human being, a testament to the genius (yet another mystery) of his creator, Sir Arthur Conan Doyle. That Holmes himself played the violin and even owned a Stradivarius made it impossible not to include the renowned detective, and of course his colleague and chronicler Dr Watson, in the investigation of the theft of del Nero's fiddle and the associated enigmas.

Already by the 1890s Victorian London, with its enormous population of over six million people, was home to an astonishingly robust and varied musical life, as documented by a brilliant and sometimes exasperating critic writing under the *nom de plume* 'Corno di Bassetto'. The Queen's Hall in Langham Place, home to the Promenade Concerts begun in 1895 under the direction of Henry J. Wood, became a leading concert venue, along with St. James's Hall, the Royal Albert Hall, Covent Garden and the Crystal Palace. Able to accommodate up to 3,000 people and characterised by excellent acoustics, it would prove to be the ideal setting for an ambitious and popular recitalist in 1901, at the dawn of a new century that was bringing with it revolutions in science, politics – and music as well. The boundaries of tonality would soon be stretched, and new genres and styles of playing were emerging. Del Nero straddles the cusp of this new world.

The Langham Hotel, a massive luxury accommodation situated close to Queen's Hall in Langham Place, would of course be the obvious choice for an artist of Del Nero's stature. Its facilities – it boasted healthy water in addition to extremely well-appointed suites that were literally fit for royalty – were incomparable. So too its guests, who included Mark Twain, Henry Wadsworth Longfellow, the explorer Henry Morton Stanley, Napoleon III, the King of Bohemia, conductor Arturo Toscanini, and composer Antonín Dvořák. Novelist Ouida (Maria Louisa Ramee) made the Langham her home and invited the likes of writers Robert Browning, Algernon Swinburne, Oscar Wilde and the adventurist Richard Burton to her 'salon'. Arthur Conan Doyle himself frequented the hotel – which he featured in three of his Sherlock Holmes tales: *A Scandal in Bohemia*, *The Sign of Four*, and *The Disappearance of Lady Frances Carfax*. The presence of a superb Erard piano made it a 'remarkably complete establishment' indeed.

Those interested in the facts providing the foundation for my tale (and an explanation of the liberties I have taken in the interests of fiction) will find a section of notes organised by chapter at its conclusion along with a selected bibliography.

Above all else however this little book is meant to delight and entertain – and in its own way to be musical itself.

Emanuel E. Garcia
Wellington
New Zealand
2009

The author wishes to express his deepest gratitude to all persons appearing in this work who though deceased have allowed themselves to be varnished, in varying degrees, by the brush of invention.

Preface

My friend Mr Sherlock Holmes has often reproached me for departing from a strictly scientific exposition of his deductive feats in favour of a narrative account characterised by 'superfluous' dramatic colour. In vain have I protested that some measure of storytelling was essential to grip and hold the reader, and that a textbook of detection, such as he planned to compose during his waning years, would fail to convey the singularity of his achievements.

In laying before the public a case that contains so many remarkable facets and that demonstrates my companion's powers at their most complex, I have merely held the mirror up to Nature, serving as scrupulous witness to a most extraordinary unfolding of events. For once Mr Holmes himself, now at his ease in the countryside of Sussex, has expressed complete satisfaction with my account.

John H. Watson, M.D.

The Langham Hotel circa 1896

Chapter One

A Dangerous Ennui

The languorous sounds of Holmes' violin floated mournfully through the brisk autumnal air of the beckoning day. The death of Moriarty had left a vacuum – not merely in the criminal underworld of London, but in my friend's scope of activity – a vacuum he was attempting to fill by a far more diligent attention to the Stradivarius he had so felicitously acquired some years before.

"Ah, Watson," he exclaimed, setting the precious instrument casually aside, "London has become drab and dull." He gestured contemptuously with his bow at a small pile of letters. "The enquiries we now receive are hardly worthy of Lestrade. How many months has it been since an interesting case has come our way?"

He recommenced playing – now a rousing and energetic air – and yet in the midst of my enjoyment I began to worry. Holmes was, if nothing else, a man of action. Not action in the crude physical sense, although to be sure he was a master of several of the arts of combat and never shirked from exerting himself while in the hunt, but action that recruited the immense talents of his marvellous brain. Without the stimulation of intellectual riddles he was prey to dangerous indiscretions. The chase was an elixir to him and he was never more himself than when matching wits with a deserving adversary. To meet the long stretches of time at his disposal he had honed his musical skills and begun even to venture into the study of fields he had previously shunned. But I wondered whether they would be enough to sustain him. Although Holmes often spoke of retiring to the country, away from the foul and putrid den of London, I could scarcely imagine it. Our lives had been intertwined for so long that the inevitable parting was painful to consider. Yet there might be benefits ...

"You would finally be able to give free rein to your considerable imagination, Watson!"

I sat up as if a gunshot had been fired.

"The novels that are straining to flow from your pen would have the time to do so," he continued.

I marvelled at the man. Many times he had astonished me by his displays of deduction, but here I was convinced that nothing short of telepathy could explain his utterance, and I told him so.

"Come now, Watson, I am forever impressed by your naive incredulity. A simple observation, followed by a trustworthy assumption – it is all so commonplace."

"Commonplace to you, Holmes, but I cannot see for the life of me how you could have read my thoughts with such accuracy. Please explain."

"And destroy the dramatic effect? Well, I suppose I must. As I was amusing myself with the fiddle I could observe you falling into a pleasant reverie – yes, I am complimented, my dear fellow – and your gaze alighted on the large new volume on the mantelpiece. It remained there – your gaze, that is – and then your countenance took on a most satisfied aspect – dreamy, in fact. Although your knowledge of German is not comprehensive, it is capable enough to translate *Traumdeutung* – the title of the book sent by the Viennese neurologist with whom I have been in correspondence. And so you dreamed a bit, my friend. I have been frank with you of late about my wish to leave the clamour of London for the cooler and quieter airs of the countryside, so it was a small step to imagine that you would be contemplating your own future, as I have been mine. While bees and music and other investigations afforded by leisure would absorb me, the writing of fiction would naturally consume your time. Indeed, it has hardly been suppressed in your chronicling of my activities."

My frown at his passing barb dissolved quickly as I lost myself in admiration of his acumen.

"And no, Watson, you need not worry about my habits. The time has come to recognise the merits of other pursuits every bit as engaging as criminal detection. Take music, for instance. I have an interest in the motets of Lassus, but the press of professional claims has until recently left me little opportunity to explore them. A proper investigation demands concentrated time without distraction. And the violin! Look, Watson, a thing of beauty, is it not? Perfect in form, crafted by a master, and yet I struggle infernally with it, doing scant justice."

A gleam of excitement suffused his restless grey eyes whenever he spoke of the violin. I anticipated another of his entertaining anecdotes about Paganini, but he tacked aslant.

"How might it sound in the hands of a true virtuoso?" he inquired wistfully.

"You sound damned good to my ears, Holmes."

"I grant you I have improved – but come, Watson, an instrument like this requires the true expert's touch. After years of disciplined application I may yet draw from it a few of the aural beauties for which it was created, but that would be far in the future. You know of course the reputation of Antonio Stradivari and his legacy. That a virtually uneducated and barely literate craftsman could fashion a miracle from a few pieces of wood, while others with far greater knowledge and resources appear to have failed – that itself is a suitable conundrum. What was his secret, Watson – the age or type of wood, the composition of varnish, the shape of the sound-holes, the contours and proportions of the violin's body? Or is it in fact a myth? Are our ears deceived and prejudiced by the Cremonese legend? One might as well attempt to understand the secrets of a woman's mind!"

Holmes was now discoursing with warmth and fervour. I for my part luxuriated in these displays of intelligence, which

19

grew in frequency as our work had fallen off. Whereas in the past Holmes had ruminated in a predictably precise manner, razor-like and directly to the point, he was now increasingly given to excursive cogitations that had no apparent governing form. Yet they were all the more delightful and surprising. He needed no encouragement to continue and leapt nimbly and effortlessly along a train of associations.

"The mind of a woman is unfathomable, Watson, and fraught with danger. Can you imagine Moriarty's genius wielded by a member of the opposite sex? I shudder at the thought, my friend, and I doubt the efficacy even of my own powers against such an opponent."

"Oh, I shouldn't worry, Holmes. Genius is the province of the male, as medical science can demonstrate. It is a simple matter of increased cranial volume. As everyone knows, all of our great scientists and thinkers are men. A female Shakespeare, for example, would be out of the question."

"And what about a female Homer, Watson?"

"Just as preposterous," I chuckled in reply.

"And yet at least one scholar of substance suggests just that."

Holmes crossed the room and retrieved a book that he thrust onto my lap: *The Authoress of the Odyssey*.

"I made the author's acquaintance during my sojourn through Italy after the incident at Reichenbach. He was gathering additional evidence for his claim that the *Odyssey* has been falsely attributed to Homer – that it was in reality composed by a woman." Holmes paused before adding with theatrical emphasis, "A woman from Trapani, Sicily."

I casually scanned the book's preface: its thesis was lamentable.

"I've never known you to take much of an interest in literature, Holmes," I said dryly and with ill-disguised disdain.

"Perhaps the idea is threatening, Watson – not my new interest in literature, but that Woman could attain the heights of literary genius?"

Holmes could become insufferably patronising at times. I might easily have thrust back: after all, it was he who was positively impervious to feminine allure, and I who had married! Nevertheless I kept admirable control of my temper and successfully denied him the satisfaction of rising to his bait. He smiled wanly, and with a trace of disappointment, I imagined.

"Will you indulge me for a moment, my friend? Dr Butler has done nothing but employ my own methods of scientific detection to literary investigation, as he frankly admitted. By the way, he implored my permission to dedicate his book to me, but I of course denied him. Public acclaim means nothing to me, as you know – least of all when it might have imperilled my actual survival, for Moriarty's accomplices were very much at large at the time and in vengeful mood."

"I am certainly grateful your name is not associated with such drivel!" I retorted.

"In some ways you are rather maddeningly conventional, my friend," replied Holmes. "At least I may thank Dr Butler for the impetus to rectify my cultural shortcomings. Now that I have perused the works attributed to Homer I find myself in agreement: the *Odyssey* bears the stamp of a woman's mind. It is as domestic as the *Iliad* is martial. And it is nothing if not a paean to deception: the wily Ulysses, man of many devices, and his even wilier wife Penelope! Man is no match for woman in the art of the lie."

"And how do you explain the Trojan horse, Holmes? Was this not a great deception? How does your theory account for *that*?" I inquired with some asperity.

"Quite readily: the story of the Trojan horse first appears in the *Odyssey*."

I turned crimson. I was ever ready to grant Holmes' superiority over me in all areas save medicine, billiards and literature. I reached for a cigar to calm my nerves and conceal my embarrassment. Holmes joined me, laying his fiddle aside, and seated himself before the fireplace. We puffed away in silence and after some moments my discomfort had dissolved altogether. I observed that Holmes had entered a meditative state – the kind that often presaged flurries of impulsive action – and I began again to be concerned.

"There are new frontiers, Watson," said Holmes dreamily. "I think often of my deceased rival – what a mind! Why, his work on the binomial theorem and the dynamics of asteroids would alone have granted him immortality. Yet for such a roving and peculiar personality mathematical science would not suffice. That he was a genius there is no doubt. But what drove him to become a mastermind of crime, Watson? Money alone cannot explain it."

"Power, my dear Holmes, it's quite simple. Of course great wealth was not unwelcome."

"But why not power for the good? No, Watson, there is something more. A mind of that type and calibre requires a particular and constant challenge, an array of subversive stimuli to keep it alive and that are as air to the lungs. Mathematics and astronomy were not scope enough for his daemon: he was too much the artist, my dear fellow, relentlessly driven to create ever more complex and macabre dramas. In fact, Watson, the great criminal and the great artist – man or woman – have much in common: they require ceaseless motion and energy, they know no laws save those they fashion for themselves, and they are masters of illusion."

Holmes brooded as the coils of smoke from his half-spent cigar made lazy spirals above his head. I regarded those noble and aquiline features in repose and shuddered to imagine how that great mind might so easily have bent itself to destructive rather than beneficent ends.

I must have drifted off briefly to sleep, for the next thing I knew Holmes was standing over me and intoning Horace's famous words as he plucked the spent cigar from my hand: "*quandoque bonus dormitat Homerus.*"

"We are both far too bored, Watson. Fortunately our tedium will be relieved when the Emperor makes his visit."

I roused myself and questioned him, for I had seen no notices in the papers and was therefore surprised and curious.

"Wilhelm or Franz Josef?"

"Neither. I am referring to a far more influential leader –
Maestro Donato del Nero, heir to Paganini: *'L'Imperatore'*, as
his witty countrymen refer to him. The emperor of the violin
and the possessor of what is reputed to be the most magical of
all the instruments to have left the great Stadivari's workshop:
the *Medici*."

"Ah yes, the concert we have booked at the Queen's Hall
on Sunday."

"Precisely, Watson. I have been keenly looking forward to
the event. It is his first appearance on our shores in over two
decades, and if rumours are to be believed, he is a changed
man – and musician. He plays at his whim, travelling
throughout the Continent and emerging unannounced at
churches and occasionally a proper hall. Nearly always, on
but a few hours' notice, the places are crowded to capacity.
His repertoire is eccentric and unpredictable and he has
apparently eschewed all association with the musical
establishment. A planned concert in a major city is for him an
anomaly. Nevertheless, if reports of his performances are true
we shall be granted an unparalleled artistic experience."

"I seem to recall that he burst upon us as a prodigy earning
universal adulation – the new Paganini and so forth – but
after a while rather suddenly disappeared. Did we not hear
him play the Beethoven concerto, and magnificently?"

"Bravo, Watson! Your memory is a good one. What a
night for the Crystal Palace! Then by his early twenties his
public performances ceased altogether. Some say he took to
drink or became mad or gambled away his earnings. Who
knows? It is only a decade since the Tuscan – he is a
Florentine, Watson – has made his great renaissance. He is
said to be the envy of every violinist of note. Mark my word,
Watson, Joachim, Ysaÿe, Sarasate, Kubelík, Hall, perhaps
even young Kreisler – every great fiddler here and on the
Continent will be in the audience."

There was comfort and reassurance for me in Holmes'
enthusiasm. His silly puns showed that the dark spell of
ennui had given way. My interest was also piqued, for
although neither a musician nor a connoisseur like my

companion, as an author I took pains to stay abreast of artistic news.

"Perhaps even more remarkably six months ago he was betrothed," continued Holmes.

"And why is this so remarkable? Some men choose to marry."

"The maestro has had a reputation with women, Watson, but not for marrying them."

"You said he was a changed man," I replied.

"Quite so, but this would be revolutionary. I worry for its effect on his artistry."

"I can assure you, Holmes, marriage is not half so bad as you imagine. My Mary was a balm to me – *and* to my medical practice."

Having ventured into what was decidedly uncomfortable terrain, for my marriage had occasionally limited my opportunities to assist him, I deftly changed the topic.

"But what about his fiddle, Holmes? How did he acquire it, and what makes it so singular, this *Medici*?"

"Mystery of mysteries, Watson. Very little is known except that it was one of a group of instruments commissioned by Grand Duke Cosimo de' Medici in the late 17th century, well before the time when Stradivari had ostensibly reached the peak of his craftsmanship. But its sound is said to be indescribable in the maestro's hands. Look here, Watson."

Holmes had beckoned me to the light where he held his own beloved Stradivarius. He had never been quite so forthcoming about his violin, a habit I attributed to the jealous guardianship of the wildly successful bargain-hunter who can scarcely believe his luck and lives in fear that his treasure will be reclaimed.

"Now, he said, carefully positioning it for illumination, "can you discern a label?"

He handed me his violin and I peered through the sound-hole.

"What do you see? Can you read it clearly?"

"Yes, wait a bit, yes." I delicately angled the violin. "It is an older script."

"Naturally. And tell me exactly what it says. Even better: here, Watson, write it out."

Holmes offered a slip of paper and, as was my wont in such matters, I took pains to ensure the utmost accuracy of my transcription, including even the violin-maker's peculiar monogram:

Antonius Stradivarius Cremonenſis
Faciebat Anno 1729

"The master's imprimatur. Thank you, Watson. And as you can see my fiddle is from Stradivari's last decade – he died in 1737. To have acquired it for a mere fifty-five shillings! Had the broker at Tottenham Court Road not been misled by the new fingerboard and elongated neck – universal modifications essential for the modern player – I would never have been so fortunate. But one sweep of the bow across its strings and there could be no doubt. I have since had it appraised by Messrs. Hill themselves, our greatest authorities, who not only confirmed its provenance but offered me a thousand guineas. I of course swore them to secrecy. It was quite careless of you, you know, to have mentioned the Stradivarius in your chronicles. Fortunately those who might be interested in acquiring it are not inclined towards the *belles lettres*."

"Just the thought of that rabble of petty London burglars ..."

"I was thinking of musicians, Watson, most of whom are far more unscrupulous and hardly more literate than your common thief."

Holmes then held his instrument aloft, its golden-brown varnish gleaming and glittering in the growing light of day, as animated and rhapsodic as a surgeon addressing an admiring group of medical students in the theatre.

"It is the genuine article, Watson," intoned Holmes with reverence. "Think what a miracle it is to transform the vibration of a string into the sweetest and most profound expression of the human soul."

I gazed at him and his treasure admiringly and then noted a subtle transformation of countenance: rapture gave way to rationalism as he moved to return the precious violin to its case, albeit with his accustomed nonchalance, for valuable though it was, he treated it with seasoned familiarity.

"As a scientist, however, I have questions. Can there be such differences in quality among well-made instruments? Are the handiworks of, for example, Vuillaume or Stainer, or for that matter, all other luthiers, so indubitably inferior to those of the Cremonese? I half-suspect that in the hands of Paganini even a trade fiddle would have sounded glorious."

Chapter Two

The Emperor Has No Violin

Our matutinal reveries were disrupted by Mrs Hudson who knocked at our door. Scarcely had Holmes called out to welcome her entry when a woman burst forth impetuously. She appeared frantic, wild with distress – and regally beautiful. She advanced upon me with an earnestness that took me aback.

"Only you can help!" she cried, taking my hand by way of supplication. The Gallic accent and smouldering dark eyes heightened the intrigue of her plea. I was speechless.

"Please, Mr Holmes, you must come to him. A terrible thing has happened!"

Holmes, his back to the window, replied.

"My good friend Dr Watson would be all too happy to assist you, but allow me the pleasure of introduction."

The unnecessary chill in Holmes' voice magnified the mystery woman's keen embarrassment.

"Then you must be Mr Holmes," she said, turning to him, and removing her hand from mine. "Oh, and you are the famous Dr Watson," she added. "I beg both your pardons." The anguish in her distraught face was almost unbearable and I was moved to great pity and concern.

"Please accommodate yourself," responded Holmes coolly. "Mrs Hudson, would you mind bringing Miss ..."

"Delumeau."

"... Delumeau some tea."

"Mr Homes, there is not time for tea. My fiancé has had his heart plucked from his breast! We must hurry!"

"Your fiancé," added Holmes rather casually.

"Yes – Signor Donato del Nero. His violin has been stolen, and Dr Watson, I am so glad that you are here, for he is in a wretched state and requires medical attention. I am desperate."

Her rich voice had fallen to a sorrowful whisper and her body became limp as a discarded puppet. Holmes sprang into action, his infectious vigour quickly reanimating Miss Delumeau.

"Come, Watson, fetch your bag," he cried with urgency, "let us make haste. A thousand pardons, Mademoiselle. Mrs Hudson, stand aside!" He retrieved his magnifying glass and walking stick and we all three hurried down the stairs and onto Baker Street where the lady's hackney was still waiting. As we settled in Holmes called out to the driver, "To the Langham, as quickly as the devil!"

Our unexpected visitor regarded Holmes with astonishment. "How did you know?"

"Where else would an emperor stay in London, especially when a piano with so fine a temperament as the Erard is available for rehearsals? Now Miss Delumeau, please tell me as much as you can. When was the *Medici* discovered to be missing?"

"So you know already of the violin, and how essential it is to my betrothed?"

"I know a little."

She seemed ready to collapse, whether from relief or from nervous exhaustion I could not tell, so I took the precaution of checking her pulse. Surely this was no time for hesitation or ceremony. The reassuring touch of a physician must have soothed her, for it was not overly rapid.

"Are you equal to the task of describing what occurred," I inquired of her, "or would you prefer to rest for now?"

Holmes glanced at me strangely and pursed his lips.

"Thank you, good doctor Watson," she replied softly. "Yes, I can go on, I *must* go on. I will tell you all I know, Mr Holmes."

"Here, this will help," I said, offering the flask of brandy I carried about for emergencies.

"Ah, thank you again, kind sir," she replied after sipping. I could feel Holmes' gaze, knowing full well that he was straining at the bit.

"I think your ministrations have been successful, Watson. Now, Miss Delumeau, if you are ready ..."

"Yes, yes." She shook her head as if to dispel confusion and her luxuriant auburn tresses spilled over the collar of her jacket.

"Donato and I arrived late last night. The journey yesterday across the Channel had been arduous, more for him, Mr Holmes, than for me, as he worried incessantly about the effect of the weather on his instrument, fearing the salt air would alter the properties of the wood. The sea was rough and the train from Dover tiresome. We both prepared for bed shortly after arriving at the Langham. I bade him good night and took refuge in my suite, which was adjacent to his. I fell asleep almost immediately. He of course carried the *Medici* with him to his rooms: he is never more than an arm's length away from the violin when we travel. Knowing him as well as I do I can assure you that he placed it just to the right of the bed ... he sleeps always on the right-hand side.

"I awoke rather early, but refreshed, and was dressing for breakfast, when of a sudden I heard an inhuman groan, one of incalculable anguish. Recognising Donato's voice and fearing the very worst – an assault, a sudden sickness, who knows? I rushed into his room. He stood as one crushed. I ran to him, happy at least to know that he was not harmed, but his body lacked all vitality. He gestured silently to the case in which his dear violin had been kept for so many years. It was on the bed and when I went to open it he snatched it away and clasped it to his breast. 'It is gone' he whispered, 'my soul, gone forever'. He then sat grasping the case, immune to my embrace, my entreaties, my endearing words, as if the spirit had fled his very body.

"I hurried frantically back to my suite to finish dressing, and only then did I realise another theft had been committed, meaningless when compared to the other, but I shuddered to imagine how."

She paused as if to gather herself while Holmes and I expectantly waited.

"Donato, in his love for me, gave me a necklace to symbolise the circle we would soon be making by our union. A string of small but exquisite pearls. I left it carelessly on my dresser before I retired, and by this morning it was gone."

"Was it valuable?" inquired Holmes.

"By whose reckoning? If you mean 'expensive', yes, quite so, but its value exceeds expense. I love him as he has never been loved, Mr Holmes, and I treasured this token of recognition. But I would sacrifice a thousand such ornaments to restore Donato's violin! We had arrived so late and so weary that I did not think to consign it to the hotel for safekeeping."

Holmes studied the refined features of that magnificent face closely, his own inscrutable to all but me. I knew that he was weighing the value of her communication and that the situation had taken on an entirely new and more complex dimension.

"Please continue," urged Holmes soothingly.

"I rang for the concierge, informed him of the thefts, of Donato's condition, and demanded he engage a physician and the constabulary. He was a kind man and promised his all, but he took me aside and strongly advised me to call upon you immediately. 'I will make sure the maestro is cared for and that his suite is left untouched until Mr Holmes arrives. His astute colleague, Dr Watson, is a medical expert and would be here as quickly as anyone else I might obtain. The police will be an unnecessary interference, at least for now. If there is anyone who can help it will be Mr Holmes'. He said this with such authority, such confidence – and of course I knew of your great reputation even on the Continent."

"Good man," chuckled Holmes. "He has saved us a world of difficulty. But tell me, was there something else, a small detail, anything you observed that struck you as odd or unusual?"

She became pensive but shook her head. "No, nothing Mr Holmes, except ..." She seemed to strain for an elusive thought and grew silent. Holmes leaned forward, his every feature on the alert.

"Why, perhaps there is ... I am not so certain, and anyway it is probably inconsequential," she added haltingly.

"I can assure you, Miss Delumeau, nothing is inconsequential. The smallest irregularity may be the portal of discovery." He could barely contain himself.

"Well, I don't know whether I was imagining things, but we passed a man along the stairway, with whom we exchanged courtesies, that is all. But I felt a chill, Mr Holmes, as if we had encountered something sinister."

"Can you describe him?" asked Holmes.

"He was tall, well-dressed, not old and yet not young. But his eyes – it was the way he looked at me, fleetingly. I have seen such a look before, but only in the worst parts of Paris."

Holmes was silent as he pondered this new information.

We drew up to the majestic Langham and were greeted by the concierge at the entrance. He took us discreetly aside.

"The maestro's condition has not changed," he reported, "and I have managed to keep everyone away. The guests know nothing, and neither do the police. My staff are with him."

"Good work, Burleigh," replied Holmes. "Now, let us make our rounds."

We strode across the commodious lobby to a wide staircase on the right and rapidly ascended to the second landing, turning east down the spacious first storey corridor until we reached the maestro's suite. Holmes bade us pause for a moment outside and issued instructions.

"Burleigh, my good man, make sure no-one enters either suite until I am through. Watson, have your medicines at the ready. Miss Delumeau, please remain at hand."

We entered quietly. Two of the hotel staff rose from their stations in the sitting room through which the maestro could be easily observed. He was, as Miss Delumeau had described, a motionless mass at the edge of his bed, clutching a battered wooden case, but obviously breathing. Holmes silently indicated that we should go no further until he had examined the premises. He did this with alacrity, moving first to the two open windows, peering outside to the left and right, then attempting to determine whether traces of entry were present on the carpet. He signalled for me to approach the maestro with his fiancée.

"Now, Miss Delumeau, see whether he will respond to you."

She delicately stroked her lover's clenched hands and gazed into his listless eyes.

"Donato, please, it is your dear Sophie! Please darling, tell me something, we are here to help," she entreated.

Her anguish and devotion were palpable.

"It is traumatic hysteria," I whispered to Holmes, "and I am afraid I will have to resort to extreme measures to disrupt the pathologic trance."

Holmes nodded in approval, and took Miss Delumeau aside. "Let us give the good doctor some room."

I positioned myself directly in front of the musician, crouching down so as to be at eye level, then addressed him thus: "Signor del Nero, at the count of three you will awaken. All will be well."

On the third count I rose and slapped the maestro hard across his cheek, knocking him backwards. The case slipped from his grasp and Holmes hastened to retrieve it, while Miss Delumeau threw herself onto her betrothed who, though smarting from the blow, was now awake and responsive. She cradled his head while I brought brandy to his lips. He was still dazed, but as soon as the alcohol reached his mouth he spat it out and looked round at the strange company that had gathered. Holmes meanwhile had opened the violin case, peering within and pausing for a moment as if to sniff. It held two bows, a velvet coverlet and an oilskin. Del Nero rose in protest but Holmes quieted him with an imperious gaze.

"Signor del Nero, I am Sherlock Holmes and this is my companion Dr Watson. We are here to assist in the recovery of the *Medici*."

"Ah, Mr Holmes," replied del Nero, a spent force, "I am most grateful." Sophie rushed back into his arms.

"Kindly remain here and gather your strength while I proceed to Miss Delumeau's suite: thieves have peculiar habits."

Holmes and I made our way to her rooms, accompanied by Burleigh. My colleague began to dart from point to point, consumed by a ferocious energy, falling now and then on his hands and knees, and using his glass. One window was open and on his way towards it he seemed to pause for a moment, as if distracted by something peculiar in the very air, and I observed a distinct change of manner. He rested his hand absently on her dresser, then continued his study, though to my accustomed eye his actions seemed now more calculated for show than substance.

We returned to the distraught and expectant couple. Holmes flung open the balcony's windows in the maestro's suite and stepped outside, examining the balustrades and ledges with scrupulous care. He returned to our midst with an air of triumph.

"Well," Holmes announced, "it is almost entirely clear to me. There remains just a trifle to complete the picture. We are dealing with a rather simple crime of opportunity. The thief had observed your entrance last night – the man who passed you in the corridor. Miss Delumeau was wearing her necklace of pearls, which he espied. It is well-known that at the Langham another element make their home – gamblers, confidence-men and the like – tut now, Burleigh, this is no time for euphemism or equivocation. Our man lay in wait. When he ascertained that you were asleep, he simply plucked your necklace from its resting place. How did he enter? Through your window: and through the same window he exited. There is a ledge that runs right round this storey and along the balconies. It was a simple thing to try his luck again by looking in on the maestro. Not finding any jewels, he spotted a curiosity, the well-worn case lying by the bed. He opened it, saw the violin ... something that could easily be pawned ... but before he could close the case again the maestro stirred. The thief hastened out through the window and along the ledge, shielded by darkness. Tell me, Burleigh, are all of the suites occupied on this storey?"

"Why no, Mr Holmes. The suite adjacent to Signor del Nero's is currently vacant."

"The final link." Holmes rubbed his palms together in satisfaction. "Through this empty suite the criminal returned to the hotel and thence to his own room."

"And the *Medici*, Mr Holmes," asked del Nero disconsolately, "is it possible to find it? Is there yet hope for me?"

Never have I seen a fellow man in such a state of mournful despair as this wretched musician who seemed on the verge of another hysterical fit.

"There is more than hope, maestro," said Holmes, "but we must act quickly. If you and Miss Delumeau would return with me now to Baker Street, I can guarantee success. I am afraid, however, that the necklace is forever out of reach. It is probably on its way to the Continent where it can fetch far more than here, for after all we Britons are not known for extravagance."

Miss Delumeau seemed utterly exhausted; only the silent entreaty of the hopeful and therefore reinvigorated del Nero convinced her to accompany us. Burleigh quickly engaged a hackney and as we alighted I observed Holmes press a slip of paper into his hand, after which the concierge whispered briefly into the detective's ear.

I for my part was simply flabbergasted. Never had I seen Holmes act with such assurance on such flimsy grounds. His theory of the crime was far from convincing, and when combined with his strange transformation in Miss Delumeau's rooms, I grew suspicious. Virtually nothing made sense. How did the thief gain access to the ledge in the first place? Why would he risk such a bold entry twice? Would it not have been easier to carry the violin in its case instead of removing it? How could Holmes be so certain that the *Medici* was not his primary target?

Chapter Three

Artistic Licence

Back at Baker Street Holmes was behaving in a most peculiar way. Mrs Hudson had prepared a table for our famished guests and during the meal Holmes was as much a servant as she, fussing about our visitors like an obsequious waiter. After we had finished he reassumed his familiar investigative airs and questioned both the violinist and his betrothed closely, eliciting however nothing new. He was uncharacteristically repetitive in his inquiries and I feared the couple, who had endured so much already, would soon be exasperated. Then when Holmes lit his pipe del Nero rose to his feet.

I take the opportunity now of describing this most eccentric of personalities. The man who, scarcely an hour before was no more than a spiritless heap, stood imperiously, living up to his moniker. He was of medium height, with the dark hair and swarthy complexion of the Italianate race. Pendulous jowls hung like dewlaps and would have had a comical effect were it not for the peculiar magnetism of his mien. His neck was short, his chest broad and his middle ample. His hands were exceptionally large with long and slender fingers. His left shoulder seemed slightly higher than his right. He was all in all a surprisingly imposing and charismatic figure, and his English, remarkably enough for a foreign speaker, bore hardly a trace of accent.

"I must protest, Mr Holmes, the use of that foul substance!

I cannot abide it. Air, Mr Holmes, air please!" he cried.

Holmes compliantly opened our windows to allow the October breeze within, and put away his tobacco.

"I see you hold strong views on one of the most pleasurable of human activities," said the detective.

"Pleasurable perhaps to those who would make a chimney of their lungs," del Nero rejoined.

"Medical science has proved the relaxing and salubrious effects of tobacco," said I, bridling at his audacity.

"I have already had a taste of your medical science, Dr Watson," del Nero glowered, lifting a hand to his cheek.

"Come now, Watson, surely our guests are entitled to courtesies," intervened Holmes diplomatically.

"Please, maestro, take your seat. You have a concert in several days' time, and even with the best of luck the *Medici* will not have been returned."

"And what am I now to do, Mr Holmes? If I cancel the engagement, not only will I suffer a substantial monetary loss but, far more important, my so-called rivals, pretenders to art and musicianship, will gloat. They will in fact accuse me of cowardice, of feigning a theft. They wish nothing better than to see this emperor become a pawn! The whole purpose for which I have made this onerous, and now disastrous, journey to this accursed island will have been for naught. Do you wish me to crawl home in shame? You see, Mr Holmes, I was lured away from the warm and glorious countryside of Tuscany for one reason: to lay to rest any doubt that as a true artist of the violin I am beyond compare."

I glanced surreptitiously at Holmes who was managing to greet these ravings with dignified composure.

"Then you must by no means cancel, maestro," advised Holmes calmly.

"And where and how and when do I find a worthy instrument? Joachim, who hoards his Stradivarii, would sooner lend me one than a miser part with gold. You miss the point altogether, Mr Holmes, for the *Medici* is as unique an instrument as I am a musician. It is the greatest of Antonio Stradivari's masterpieces, and only with the *Medici* may I enter the heavens."

"What greater triumph than to best your jealous rivals without it? I have heard the whispers ... that the *Medici* is bewitched, that your playing is utterly dependent upon its magical powers and that without it you are a journeyman." Holmes' tone was cool, nonchalant.

"Preposterous!" exploded del Nero, reddening. "I can take the cheapest fiddle of the lowliest student and surpass them!" He shook visibly. I had heard, and read, much about the artistic temperament, but never had I occasion to observe such a demonstration *in vivo*.

"Well," said Holmes deftly presenting his own Stradivarius, "do you think this might be a suitable substitute? If not I am sure that Messrs. Hill would be honoured to lend you one of their own."

Del Nero, his frenzy now abated, accepted the violin with deliberate grace. His eyes and hands moved adroitly in appraisal. He peered through the sound-holes and Holmes was on the point of offering his magnifying lens when he realised it was not in his possession.

"Ah, now I remember – I left it on that accursed balcony. I will send Mrs Hudson for it at once, with your permission, Maestro."

"Yes, by all means," responded del Nero, preoccupied with scrutinising Holmes' violin. Holmes left us briefly to trespass further upon Mrs Hudson's good graces.

"It appears to be genuine, Mr Holmes," announced del Nero on Holmes' return.

"I can assure you it is despite rumours to the contrary which I for obvious reasons have not discouraged."

"May I confirm?" asked del Nero. "Ah, a bow of John Dodd – excellent, Mr Holmes, second only to Tourte."

Del Nero rose with violin and bow. Without ceremony he began to play – I know not what – but in less than a minute he had woven a musical spell such as I had never before experienced, summoning a cascade of emotion from the breasts of his auditors. The maestro's fingers flew across the instrument sounding notes that tested the full range of its compass, and drawing from it a sound uncannily sweeter and more powerful than I had ever heard. Such strange enchanting wondrous music, what touches of sweet harmony! Holmes' earnest face glowed with admiration and satisfaction. There was no question: del Nero was a master. The violinist stopped abruptly, wrenching us from our dreams.

"A fine instrument, Mr Holmes," he said matter-of-factly, "and I commend you for not following the ridiculous custom of Spohr's." He paused, pondering his choices. "Of course, it cannot compare with the *Medici*, and I will sadly not be able to ascend Olympus. But 'tis enough, 'twill serve. You are correct, Mr Holmes: my triumph will be all the greater. It is like ... how do you call it in horse-racing?"

"A handicap!" I exclaimed.

"Yes, a handicap, just as you say, Dr Watson. My victory will be the sweeter for the extra burden I carry. But I have not a moment to lose: I must get to know the violin, and it me, in the briefest of intervals. If we are fortunate it will be like a torrid love affair between parties who meet for a time and know they can never meet again. I speak of course figuratively, my dear Sophie."

"It is an honour to lend it to you, maestro," said Holmes, "but I must impose a condition."

Del Nero regarded Holmes with apprehension.

"I ask only that you return my Stradivarius personally each evening and that you join me in a glass of claret."

Del Nero burst into relieved laughter, but almost as quickly grew sombre.

"Can you really reclaim my true love, Mr Holmes, are you certain she is not lost forever?"

"I am expecting news tonight, maestro: my minions have been placed on the alert. Ah, I see that Mrs Hudson has already returned and will have my lens. Would you care to inspect the label more closely?"

"There is no need, Mr Holmes," del Nero answered with majestic dismissal. "Come, my dearest," he directed his fiancée.

Sophie Delumeau, poor woman, was evidently overwrought. As she parted she pressed my hand warmly, and said in a weak but tender voice, "I am so grateful, Dr Watson."

What an odd pair, I mused, and how long would her youth and beauty endure?

"Until tonight, maestro," called Holmes.

Scarcely had they exited when Holmes addressed me conspiratorially.

"What is your preference, Watson?"

"A cigar would be most welcome."

"Indeed!"

We puffed away silently for some minutes, luxuriating in the much-needed refreshment.

"It clarifies one's thinking, does it not?"

"Indubitably, my dear Holmes."

"A wonder the maestro is so opposed. A strange man, no?"

"More than strange. He suffers from megalomania, if you ask me. And the way he treats Miss Delumeau ... why, she could hardly say a word in his presence. How in the world does she manage to sing?" I added.

"She has already begun to make a name for herself in the smaller houses, Watson. A powerful and pure voice, I am told. But the maestro is no more a megalomaniac than any other virtuoso of the violin. The demands of that most demanding of instruments, and the infinite perfectibility of music cannot be met by a timid personality."

"Do you really think you can help him, Holmes? Your reconstruction of the crime did not persuade me," I added boldly.

"No? And have you formed your own theory?"

"Not yet, I am awaiting further evidence. But I suspect the entire affair is a murky and complicated one."

"Very good, Watson, you outdo yourself. As the evidence accrues, kindly let me know any further valuable ideas. And as to your other question, yes, I believe I can help Signor Donato del Nero, and it is time that I made some inquiries."

* * * * *

41

Holmes strolled in casually just after evening had fallen. I watched him closely for signs of progress, but he seemed deliberately uncommunicative. He proceeded to air our modest rooms in preparation for the musician's visit. Del Nero and Miss Delumeau arrived shortly thereafter, keenly expectant.

"Have you any news, Mr Holmes?" began del Nero breathlessly.

"Yes, maestro, and good news at that. I have been able to trace your beloved *Medici*."

Holmes protected himself from an imminent assault of Italian gratitude – the crushing embrace, the kissing of cheeks and hands and so forth – by the mere authority of his voice.

"I have traced it, maestro, but I can say no more except that it will be returned on the evening after your concert. And that if your concert does not take place, you will never see it again."

Del Nero stood incredulous, a study in apoplexy, as if smitten by an unseen and unjust enemy against whom he had no recourse.

"Why this is blackmail! I will not stand for it! We must employ the police!" he thundered.

"We must do nothing of the sort, maestro," replied Holmes calmly.

"How much do they want? I have money, Mr Holmes," he urged.

"That will not be necessary. Apparently you have been challenged and your foe has interests other than lucre. You have been handicapped, maestro."

Del Nero's incendiary Italian temper could no longer be restrained.

"The fools! They will lose, Mr Holmes, they do not know my true value. Sarasate, that ignoramus – he must be behind this, or Ysaÿe, that cunning impostor, or perhaps that so-called 'violinist to the Queen': she is as duplicitous as the others. They shall see, those scoundrels, of what mettle I am made!" The musician shook with ungovernable fury.

Miss Delumeau, paler and more nervous than in the morning, nonetheless hastened to assuage del Nero. Her touch was a soothing one, and when he had eventually settled and gathered himself he was able to relate that his work with Holmes' violin had gone exceedingly well. He graciously thanked Holmes as he handed it over.

"Yes, we are getting acquainted, it is going nicely," the becalmed virtuoso continued. "My accompanist mistook it at first for my *Medici*, but he is a Russian and is only just returning to music after a mental collapse. In any case, Mr Holmes, you could do me a great favour by playing. It would help me to understand how it has been used as I strive to accustom it to my own sonorities and style."

For the first and only time in our long and intimate association, Holmes blushed.

"Come, Mr Holmes, a few minutes at most. It would be extremely helpful," urged Del Nero.

Holmes, regaining composure, acquiesced. I confess I took no little joy at the sight of his discomfort.

"What shall I attempt, maestro?" asked Holmes timidly.

"Anything, anything so long as it is not scales or arpeggios. Some real piece of music please."

After a nearly interminable amount of throat-clearing, the positioning and repositioning of the violin and the tuning and fine-tuning of every string, Holmes finally assayed the Hoffmann *Barcarolle*, a rather dependable choice for my friend whose adventurous instincts for improvisation had deserted him. Del Nero listened, opening his eyes only occasionally. A ring of perspiration decorated Holmes' brow by the time he had finished.

"Bravo, Mr Holmes, for an amateur you are not half bad. Let me guess: you began playing rather late, at the age of ten or eleven. It is evident from the deficiencies of your left hand: the lightning quickness and subtleties are not there. They are irremediable, but not fatal. Ideally one should begin study by the age of four at the very latest, but no matter. Your bowing is exceptional, though you do not play often enough and a certain coarseness can be heard when you begin and end a phrase. Your intonation, however, is surprisingly excellent. And you have style, Mr Holmes, that is clear – and unteachable. In short, with several years of assiduous practice, a chair in the second violin section of a rural English orchestra would be within reach. But of course your temperament would not allow you to suffer such an ignoble fate. You choose merely to entertain yourself, or to amuse the masses at your local tavern with Scottish airs. May I make a suggestion? When you practice, devote some time to playing very slowly and very softly. You will find it works wonders. And eventually, who knows? You may yet justify possession of such an instrument. On the whole your playing has not hurt it, and that is saying a great deal. So I say to you, Mr Holmes, bravo!"

Holmes bowed for lack of knowing how else to respond to such effrontery. Yet it was sobering to hear an expert's unvarnished assessment. Del Nero was neither harsh nor inaccurate but offered his comments as a realist, and in good faith.

"What time will you require the violin tomorrow maestro?" inquired Holmes meekly.

"Nine o'clock. I practice six hours daily, no more. In the early morning I perform my Swedish exercises. Musicians are athletes, Mr Holmes – your medical science should tell you this, Dr Watson – athletes of the fine musculature, but we must also keep our large muscles in form."

Suddenly del Nero leapt to his feet to show us a sample of his regimen, running in place, hopping from foot to foot, waving his arms about, bending and twisting his torso and so forth. His spirits were evidently much improved. He and Miss Delumeau took their leave shortly after this display, and Holmes fairly ran to the mantelpiece to fetch his pipe whilst I clipped a cigar.

"Artistic licence?" I inquired.

"Artistic licence," sighed Holmes, settling peacefully into his armchair.

Chapter Four

A Demoiselle in Distress

The next day dawned crisp and clear and Holmes strolled to the Langham to deliver his violin into the eager and waiting hands of the 'Emperor.'

"The maestro had just finished his exercise regimen," chuckled Holmes. "The day is a fine one, bright with hope, though you can be sure that London is teeming with intrigue."

"No doubt," I answered, casting a querying eye his way. "Speaking of which, how the devil did you manage to track down the *Medici* so quickly? Can you really be so certain of its return?"

Before he could respond footfalls were heard on the stair.

"Miss Delumeau, if I am not mistaken," noted Holmes. "I was expecting her."

It was indeed Sophie Delumeau, radiant and beautiful, but harried by nerves. She glanced at me and smiled and I rose in greeting. Her eyes flickered my way in tumult as Holmes ushered her in with his natural suavity.

"Miss Delumeau, would you care for …

"No tea, Mr Holmes, thank you."

"Pray, how may I help you this morning, Mademoiselle?"

Her graceful hands fluttered restlessly like wayward moths and her breathing was irregular. Then of a sudden she fell into a stillness and sat as if in reverie, signalling to my medical acumen an imminent nervous attack. I hastened to her side with brandy, which she gratefully accepted, and I could not help but regard Holmes with reproach for his impassivity in the face of such distress.

"For this relief, good Dr Watson, much thanks. It seems that Mr Holmes is less moved by the plight of human suffering."

"A scientist must preserve his objectivity, Miss Delumeau," replied Holmes, "and in any case Dr Watson has compassion to spare."

She lifted her warm large eyes, accentuated by stress and pallor, to the detective, and spoke quietly.

"Do you know of the Baroness Helene von Dobeneck, Mr Holmes?"

"A friend of Paganini's, I believe."

"A friend of Paganini's." She paused as if meditating upon those words which she had repeated with deliberation. "Yes, I suppose you are correct. She was indeed a friend, Mr Holmes, but she was also much, much more. Will you condescend to listen?"

"Listening is never a condescension for me, Miss Delumeau. Pray proceed at your leisure."

"Thank you, kind sir," she rejoined provocatively. "Helene von Dobeneck was an extraordinary woman, a woman of many talents and many dimensions. She hailed from a distinguished family: her father, Professor Feuerbach, was knighted by the Bavarian court for his work in jurisprudence. One brother became a philosopher, one an archaeologist, and another a mathematician. Yet she was the most gifted of all, and beautiful, Mr Holmes, although I suppose that would hold no interest for you. Unfortunately she was compelled to enter into a loveless alliance with the Baron von Dobeneck.

"In 1829 she chanced to hear Paganini in Nuremberg. Such was the soul she possessed that she could divine from the capricious displays of empty virtuosity a true, a great and a magnificent artist. And it was with the artist she fell in love."

Miss Delumeau paused, her eyes flashing as if in defiance.

"She did not love half-way, Mr Holmes. Her devotion was genuine and limitless. She had the courage to divorce the

Baron and invite scorn, scandal and penury, wanting nothing more than to dedicate herself to Paganini: she eschewed his wealth and wished only for his hand. He, scoundrel that he was, fled the only true love aside from his mother's that he would ever know, casting aside a woman far above him in social standing, a woman who had sacrificed everything. When he left for Paris without her and she recognised that the love he promised was ephemeral, she broke down utterly. But after a time of recovery she too moved to that great city to cultivate her voice under the auspices of the peerless Manuel Garcia and, no doubt, to wait for the impossible. She was an exceptional singer yet she shunned a beckoning career on the operatic stage. She remained in Paris for a decade, painting, composing, singing, but above all hoping secretly and fervently that Paganini would someday return to her.

"He did not, Mr Holmes. Ten years after they first met he died without ever having seen her again. Helene collapsed upon hearing the news and was sent to a sanatorium. After she was released she literally threw herself into the arms of a monk and converted to Roman Catholicism, the religion into which her faithless lover had been born, seeking refuge in a Benedictine convent. Her agitated soul could not be sufficiently assuaged by holy orders so she did not take her final vows, becoming instead a recluse and a pilgrim wandering across the Continent, finding temporary homes in Zurich and Rome before meeting her end in Treviso at the age of eighty.

"And yet, Mr Holmes, one may understand Paganini's actions even while deploring them. How could he have married a woman whose affection would have been an unending reproach to his very livelihood? For she did not fall in love with the buffoon of the violin who imitated the sounds of animals, or who played trick pieces on a single string. No, Helene was drawn to the genuine man, the incomparable artistry of the private Paganini, an artistry never revealed to the public, not even when he played gratis at the cemetery of the Lido.

"This is why I have come today, Mr Holmes, to tell you something even you do not, cannot know. The public Paganini played a Guarnerius violin – the *Cannon* – and on this he mimicked the braying of a donkey, or the call of a bird, the squawk of an old woman, all to the delight of the vulgar. On the *Cannon* he used his scordatura, performed those insipid duets on the G and E strings alone, and astonished with his technical bravura. For Paganini the stage was not a place where Beethoven, Mozart, Haydn, or even his own *Capricci* might appear. No, it was merely a platform for extravagant showmanship, petty theatricalities, promiscuous adulation … and artistic death. Only in private would the musician emerge to render with honest beauty the works of the masters. And for these intimate encounters with the sublime he relied not on the *Cannon*, but on an instrument whose expressive palette had no equal."

Miss Delumeau was sombre but alert. The cadences of her voice and the story that unfolded had a mesmerising effect.

"Imagine, Mr Holmes, and you too, my dear Dr Watson, the choice with which Paganini was faced: to love and be loved as he had never been, as indeed he could hardly dare to have imagined, and consequently to realise himself as an artist in the most noble manner, or to continue with his endless and meretricious public charades. He chose the latter, of course, and yet he knew better within his bosom and attempted to redeem himself: he left Helene a singular gift, something through which his essence and the love therein could be symbolised. She cherished this inimitable remembrance and carried it with her throughout her wanderings. On her deathbed in her Spartan apartment in Treviso she was found clutching it to her breast. They say her face was serene."

"The *Medici*," murmured Holmes.

"Yes, the *Medici*," she responded with gravity. "All those years, Mr Holmes, her love had burned true! And in her testament she left instructions to bestow the violin only upon the worthiest of artists, one possessed of unparalleled skill on the instrument, but who would employ that skill in the service of the ideals of music rather than sell his birthright for the pottage of virtuosic display.

"By a miracle my Donato came to possess this very violin – he will tell you himself – and has grown into a Prometheus. He depends upon it for his very breath and with it he bequeaths to his auditors the gift of light and unsuspected realms. If it is not recovered, Mr Holmes ..."

She levelled a hard unstinting gaze at my companion during a silence that seemed endless, before resuming finally in hushed tones.

"I first heard Donato play in Paris last year, at the church of Saint Louis en L'Île. In his violin there was everything that I as a singer had striven for ... and more, much more. I recognised at once his genius. How could I not have fallen so thoroughly and divinely in love? I had a beau at the time: to break his heart was horrible but necessary, *pauvre homme*. But the months with Donato since our engagement have been blissful, despite the increasing number of performances and this mad venture here. Why he should journey to a land he detests when he is above all competition and has nothing to prove is beyond me."

She shrugged as if to imply that del Nero was entitled to his whims, and then smiled.

"Thank you, gentlemen, and good day."

After the remarkable Sophie Delumeau had departed, I turned to Holmes expectantly. "Most interesting" was all he could muster, oblivious to the consternation that was impossible for her to conceal as she took her leave.

"And now, my dear fellow," declared Holmes, "there is a most pressing errand to which I must attend." His nonchalance was positively exasperating.

* * * * *

I reflected on the sequence of disquieting events. Holmes was evidently not himself – that I could easily gather from his uncharacteristically mundane explanation of the crime and his unwarranted confidence that a valuable object, in the hands of criminals, could reliably be retrieved. In the past such aberrations meant that Holmes was pursuing a separate line of inquiry. I comforted myself that I too could apply the principles of deduction to puzzling matters. I remembered two curious incidents whose singularity warranted study: Holmes' secreting a message to the Langham's concierge, Burleigh, and then his 'forgetting' his magnifying glass and despatching poor Mrs Hudson to retrieve it. I reasoned that the note to Burleigh and Mrs Hudson's mission were linked. But how?

First a cigar! I had settled back into my chair and went once again through the entire chain of events, pausing at each juncture simply to ponder in as relaxed and meditative a manner as possible. To my surprise it took scarcely a moment before everything became impressively clear: the violin must be at the Langham still! Only thus, I reasoned, could Holmes be so confident. My friend had given Burleigh instructions to secure the hotel by engaging Lestrade's men to keep steady watch. Despite their lack of imagination the men of Scotland Yard had at least the virtues of doggedness and consistency and could be counted upon for diligence. And in addition Holmes, I am sure, would have deployed his Irregulars. When Mrs Hudson returned yesterday morning with his glass, she had borne tidings from Burleigh that his instructions had been carried out. How could I have overlooked the obvious for so long?

Somewhere in that palatial hotel the criminal, and the *Medici*, were to be found. It was important however not to alarm him – hence Holmes' slapdash theory and his whisking us away from the scene. A brilliant move on his part, for the villain would remain at his ease – and at the Langham. That the inspiration for the strategy struck him while in Miss Delumeau's rooms was now beyond doubt, as this would explain the sudden change of manner I had observed at the time.

So there it was – Holmes had ascertained in a flash that the thief had returned to his room at the hotel and he was now simply biding his time before he pounced. A cat and mouse game, but a perilous one, for a false move meant that the *Medici* could be lost forever.

My spirits rose as I gained such insight. Holmes would be impressed by my reasoning, but I was determined to play my cards close to my chest for now. I was troubled too by possibilities. What if Lestrade's men suffered a lapse, and if Holmes' urchins proved unreliable? It was then that I spied her glove – Miss Delumeau's – resting nearly invisibly upon the chair she had only moments ago vacated. Strange – how could she forget it? The morning was brisk and she would have noted its absence within minutes and returned for it – so said 'reason'. There must be more. The glove was a signal – not to Holmes whose coolness lent itself to distrust, but to me. I after all had twice come to her aid as she was on the verge of breakdown. From Holmes, preoccupied as he was with the machinations of deduction, there was little in the way of human sympathy.

I thus determined to act. If the glove had been carelessly forgotten, there would certainly be no harm in my returning it. But if it were deliberately placed, then it would be incumbent upon me to discover what Sophie Delumeau was attempting to communicate.

I arrived at the Langham in short order and asked for Miss Delumeau. The brightness with which she greeted me confirmed my suppositions. She thanked me abundantly and then suggested we take tea. I was intent upon making all seem as natural as possible in case our meeting should be remarked upon.

"Doctor Watson," she said, "your honest face is a balm to my soul. I know beyond doubt I can trust you and that I may confide in you. You recall the man I mentioned on the stairs the night we arrived?" Her voice lowered to a whisper. "I fear he is still here."

"Yes, I suspected as much," I replied conspiratorially, "but do not worry. Mr Holmes moves in mysterious ways his wonders to perform, Mademoiselle, and he has kept us all in the dark, but I now know for certain that he has laid a delicate but inescapable trap."

51

She fixed me with dark and searing eyes.

"And can you be so sure he will succeed? You see, Dr Watson, your friend is a man of intellect, of the brain; but he is not a man of the heart. The heart is a far more discerning organ. You, doctor, know about hearts ... as a physician and as a man, of that I am certain."

"We must be circumspect, Miss Delumeau. Where have you seen him?"

"I have not seen him, Dr Watson, I do not need to see him: but I can *feel* his presence. As I was coming to you today I was overtaken by it, a sense of evil, a malicious force that was unmistakable. He is here, Doctor, beyond doubt, but only someone who has the heart to perceive will know. To your Mr Holmes, to the entire detective force of London he will pass as a gentleman, indiscernible among the many. But not to you. I have perhaps said too much. Forgive me, and thank you so very much for your great kindness. I must be going."

She hastened away abruptly as if embarrassed, and I lingered at the table nonplussed, absently finishing my tea while pondering her words and her appeal for help. I wondered did the maestro realise what a treasure he was about to possess in marriage! As I myself rose a man moving quickly and furtively caught my eye. He was tall, well-dressed, and carried a small package under his left arm, but as his back was towards me I could not discern his face. A shudder coursed through my limbs, my scalp began to tingle and I was overcome by an almost indescribable *frisson* that recalled my experiences of the battlefield in Afghanistan: sickness, evil and malice all in concentrated combination. No, my heart did not err.

I shook off the uncanny paralysis that had begun to beset me and made my way towards the stranger as inconspicuously as possible, down the main staircase and through the bustling foyer. He was now outside the hotel. I hurried towards him, fighting both the crowd and the lingering debility of my war wounds. He, however, was lean and his step was devilishly quick. Where were Lestrade's forces? To my dismay I saw that he was gaining on me and on the very verge of escape, on the brink of eluding Holmes' carefully constructed web! I had no choice but to call upon my reserves and break into a run. I flung myself onto the unsuspecting criminal with all the strength of which I was capable, taking as much care as possible to protect the violin he was spiriting away. Yet the force of my tackle caused the bundle inadvertently to shoot from his arms, and I watched with indescribable sadness and horror as it was crushed by the wheels of a passing hansom.

Chapter Five

The Fate of the *Medici*

"**D**amn you, Watson," hissed an all too familiar voice, "can I not buy cigars in peace? Thanks to you we've lost a hundred of the finest – Cuban no less!"

Holmes brushed himself off and I stood chagrined and aghast at my error. Fortunately the cigars could be easily, if expensively, replaced, and Holmes had sustained merely a minor bruise. He stopped my stream of apologies and simply urged me to allow him the pleasure of taking in the sights of the great city on a particularly splendid day. No dressing down in the military could have made me feel as crestfallen as the amused twinkle of Holmes' grey eyes. An audience of passers-by, of which I had been oblivious, added to my dismay.

"Facts, Watson, facts," he called out to me as we parted, "they are indispensable. Till evening, my friend."

Bowed but not broken, I sought the refuge of my club where I idled away at billiards before returning to our quarters.

The maestro and Miss Delumeau had anticipated my rather late arrival. Claret was being served and the maestro was buoyant.

"Yes, Mr Holmes, we are becoming fast friends, your fiddle and I. Sophie, poor darling, is worried about the *Medici*, but I have told her that you are an artist, and that from one great artist to another there can only be trust and confidence, no? When you say that my matchless violin will be returned I believe you as firmly as I believe in my dear Sophie's love."

"Your faith in me is much appreciated, Signor del Nero," replied Holmes as he darted a glance my way, "but I rather think of myself as a scientist first and foremost."

"Your science and your scientific principles are the foundation of your art, to be sure. We know all of us, even on the Continent, of your discovery and vanquishing of the foul Professor Moriarty. Scotland Yard had your facts, Mr Holmes, your multitudinous facts about crime, but it was your artistry that saw beyond them and led you to this villain who, invisible to them, masterminded a vast web of criminal activity that stretched far beyond London. So, my dear Mr Holmes, a great scientist must be an artist, and a great artist a scientist."

"The maestro is perfectly correct, Holmes," added I. "It is the same in medicine. The astute physician is one who can see beyond a bewildering array of symptoms to divine the illness beneath: there is an art of medicine founded on the science."

"Just as in violin-making," added del Nero emphatically. "To think that within a minute's walk of the Piazza San Domenico in Cremona were the workshops of the masters, clustered together: Bergonzi, Storioni, Ruggeri, Amati, Guarneri, and of course, Stradivari. Their art and their science have yet to be equalled."

"On that score I suppose we are in full agreement," smiled Holmes.

Sophie sat quietly, flashing occasionally an uneasy glance my way.

"I hear that you have learned of the Baroness von Dobeneck from Sophie, and the role of Paganini. He is a man by whom I am both cursed and blessed. Cursed by the endless and unjustifiable comparisons the peasantry insist on making between him and me. The 'new Paganini' and such nonsense. I am as much the new Paganini as you are the new Dupin, Mr Holmes! Like all Italians, Paganini could not help but play the clown, and he was richly rewarded for it. He used the violin as an instrument of crude entertainment, mimicking the cries of the animal kingdom and the sounds of other instruments, playing sonatas on one string, using the scordatura and harmonics for spectacular effects. Only his intimates knew of the artist that existed behind the mask of the comedian. Only his dearest friends heard the Mozart and Haydn he could command, the Beethoven quartets he could infuse with his incomparable skill and sensitivity. And only Helene, *povera donna*, would love him truly and deeply, this man who could not help but betray her as he betrayed himself.

"You know already how Helene came to possess the *Medici*, but not how fate smiled upon me. To tell you of my fortune I must first tell you what I know of the *Medici's* provenance."

Holmes refilled our glasses, brimful of exuberant interest and anticipation.

"In 1684 the Marchese Bartolommeo Ariberti ordered from Antonio Stradivari a group of instruments for the court of the Grand Duke of Tuscany, Cosimo III de' Medici. It was the same year that Stradivari's teacher Amati had died. Six years later, in 1690, two violins and a violoncello were presented to His Highness, and their reception was such that immediately the two violas necessary to complete the concerto were commissioned.

"In 1794 one of the violins was sold by a Florentine, Signor Mosell, and eventually made its way to your Mr Hill of London, thanks to whom I was enabled to sample its charms. It is known as the *Tuscan* and is a remarkably fine instrument. The cello and a viola are in Florence still; however the second viola has never been found. The other violin was thought to be lost as well, but this had become the property of Paganini, and then his lover Helene.

"You must remember, Mr Holmes, that not only do Italians have a reputation for comedy, but also for theft. After the demise of the Duchy in 1734, many valuable possessions were improperly removed. A rich Florentine businessman had somehow managed to acquire the *Medici*. He himself was an amateur musician, but when he heard the Genoese play he was possessed by a fit of uncharacteristic good-will and simply pressed it upon Paganini, who brought it to Vuillaume for the usual repairs and alterations: a raised and lengthened neck, new fingerboard, tailpiece and reinforced bass-bar, and of course a freshly cut and fitted bridge. As Sophie has already revealed to you, Paganini did not use this instrument in public, but, having discovered its miraculous properties, employed it solely for the sake of genuine music, in secrecy.

"He must have been tempted, Mr Holmes, by that magnificent violin, tempted to abandon his chicanery and realise himself as artist rather than harlequin. But by then he was old beyond his years, and dogged by illness, unable to change or perhaps unwilling. No one can know.

"Yet his profound allegiance to the creative ideal cannot be in doubt, as his singular gift to Hector Berlioz attests – an act of supreme and unparalleled generosity among artists. I have committed to memory the words of his immortal letter."

Mio caro amico,

Beethoven spento, non c'era che Berlioz che potesse farlo rivivere; ed io che ho gustato le vostre divine composizioni, degne di un genio qual siete, credo mio dovere di pregarvi a voler accettare in segno di mio omaggio, ventimila franchi ...

Del Nero had lapsed unawares into his native language, then recovered himself. "Ah, my friends," he exclaimed, emerging as if from a spell, "permit me to translate."

> My dear friend,
>
> Beethoven being dead, only Berlioz can make him live again; and I who have savoured your divine compositions, worthy of the genius you are, believe it is my duty to beg you to accept, as a token of my homage, twenty thousand francs ...

"These twenty-thousand francs to the impoverished Berlioz – they saved his life! Without Paganini there would have been no symphony of *Romeo and Juliet*. Yet this was the very same man who scorned to perform the immortal *Harold in Italy*, which he himself commissioned, because there were too many rests in the solo part! Truly a man of contradictions, as are we all I suppose.

"The gift to Helene, however, of the most superb violin he would ever own or play was even more magnanimous: it was a testament to the ideals of love he could never attain, and an acknowledgment of her ability to fathom his better soul.

"There is a story about this fated instrument, the *Medici*. At the Tuscan Court was a superb violinist, Gesualdo da Rimini, who was also a hunchback. To him was granted the privilege of using the new Stradivarius violin, which was quite different from its brother the *Tuscan*. It was an allongé Stradivarius, longer than the classic model on whose lines the *Tuscan* had been constructed. The *Medici* is a full fourteen and five-sixteenths inches instead of the usual fourteen, and the body of the instrument is changed to accommodate this length: the bouts are less curved, the sound-holes a bit wider. Its tone is powerful and sonorous, and its timbre rich and dark, as I trust you will hear in a few days' time.

"Well, when da Rimini played, he moved the denizens of the earth as well as the heavens. The beautiful wife of a nobleman was carried away and she arranged for a private concert at his modest home. It was so successful, and she so oblivious to Gesualdo's deformity, that another was planned. But this time da Rimini's violin had only three strings: the fourth had been used around his neck. His mistress, in the midst of her distress upon discovering the corpse, snatched the fiddle and sequestered herself in a convent. She refused to surrender the instrument, and the Church intervened so that she would not be molested so long as she remained within the confines of her new home. Over time she taught herself to play a little and the rudimentary but sweet sounds she was able to produce graced the devotions of her community. She eventually withered away from heartbreak and upon her death the *Medici* was returned to the Tuscan court. It is said that Cosimo himself was responsible for its preservation, as her husband was bent on destroying it. No musician, however, would touch it as it possessed by now a reputation for sorcery and danger. It lay unused, a magnificent museum-piece around which the wildest of superstitions grew.

"Just over ten years ago, Mr Holmes, I was approached by a cleric. Sincerity and wisdom were engraved upon his face. The wide expanse of a noble forehead and deep-set eyes marked him as a man of piety. He 'chanced' to hear an impromptu concert I had given in Venice, at the Church of San Nicoló al Lido, and he approached me afterwards and engaged me in a most fascinating conversation relating the motions of heavenly bodies to the harmonies produced by the violin. I was at that time playing an Amati which, though beautiful in every way, prevented my ascending the heights to which I aspired. Man's reach should always exceed his grasp, Mr Holmes, but in my case I knew the distance was far greater than warranted.

"He invited me to luncheon the next day and as we broke bread together he spoke of a most unusual mission he had undertaken, a mission, said he, which had reached its culmination in our meeting.

"Needless to say, I was deeply perplexed and I pressed him to explain himself. It was then that he related the history of Helene von Dobeneck neè Feuerbach, Paganini's gift, and her last Will and Testament. Even before her death in 1888 the good Father Grancevola, for so was he named, had been charged by Helene to find a musician worthy of the *Medici*. To such an end he had followed closely the careers of violinists throughout the Continent and often travelled long distances to sample their talents, venturing even to your British Isles. He sought a musician without pretence, one wholly dedicated to the ideals of interpretive expression above all; one whose profound technical skill was placed in the service of music rather than self-display.

"For years he roamed widely but discovered that vanity far exceeded musicianship, which of course is hardly a surprise. He was on the verge of despairing that the Baroness's wishes would ever be realised when fate led him to my concert in Venice and, Mr Holmes and Dr Watson, I do not exaggerate to say that he could scarcely describe the effect of my playing upon his sensitive soul. I had rendered Bach that evening, the D-minor partita without a break. The Lord, said the good Father, had blessed him and now his waiting had not been for nought. He had brought the *Medici* with him and literally begged me to play it to confirm his judgment.

"As we were close to the church of the Madonna dell 'Orto, we repaired to its courtyard. At his request I performed once again the gigue from the partita, and I swear to you upon the grave of my mother that Father Grancevola fell to his knees in tears. I joined him and we both of us embraced, sobbing together, for I could feel in communing with this instrument such expressive power and such felicity of tone and timbre as could hardly be imagined despite its years of idleness. My hand shook as I held this gift from the gods. Only a miracle could account for my raising it from the dead!

"'Take it,' he said, 'and I ask only two things so that the testament of the Baroness may be honoured. You must never play in Treviso, nor visit her church, San Gaetano da Thiene, of which I am pastor, as she wishes her soul to be left in peace. You are to make a donation to me no later than tomorrow, of a sum of your choosing, which I will pledge to the care of the impoverished of our flock in accordance with the Baroness's directives. I will meet you here tomorrow at noon. Tonight I sing praises to the Lord'.

"I held the *Medici* in my trembling hands and rushed back to my hotel. I inspected it closely: it was magnificent, its reddish-brown hue was captivating to the eye, and its sound – it cannot be described. I played upon it for hours that evening and I could feel within myself grow an ability to transcend the very music I interpreted. The instrument was peerless.

"The next day I met with my benefactor. He had me sign a document stipulating the conditions set forth by the Baroness about Treviso, a trifling formality. And then I had the pleasure of bestowing upon him an amount that would have fetched a dozen Stradivarii on the open market. I gave of it freely, Mr Holmes, and I have been repaid a thousandfold, though not in Caesar's worldly coin. Not without tears did we bid each other adieu.

"Since then for these past ten years the *Medici* has hardly left my side. We have grown together: my sonorities have shaped it, and it has in turn shaped me by its response. Many times have I been tempted to journey to Treviso if only to pay homage to the memory of the Baroness and thanks to that kindly emissary of fate, the good Father Grancevola, if indeed he is still alive. But I am a man of honour. Now perhaps you can understand the condition in which you found me at the hotel. To have my heart wrenched from me unawares ... it was too much to bear."

Sophie Delumeau reached over and stroked his arm. He kissed her hand in return.

"It is growing late, Donato," murmured that fine woman.

"Yes, my dear, another full day lies ahead. I shall expect you at the same time tomorrow, Mr Holmes. My gratitude is profound, as is my confidence in your abilities, your word, and your Stradivarius as well. Good night, Dr Watson."

As Holmes and I smoked our last cigars of the day – I had replenished our stock to make amends for my blunder – I gave an account of my meeting with Sophie Delumeau, laying emphasis on her premonition of danger.

"I fear it is not entirely unjustified, Watson," responded Holmes to my surprise, as I had expected disagreement and dismissal. "A life devoted to art is a most dangerous one," he added solemnly, "and there are complexities I had not anticipated."

Holmes did not elaborate, preferring instead to turn the troubles of his countenance merely upon himself. I was too weary and too perplexed to press him further about the incongruities of the case and its growing mystery. As I took my leave he sat gazing absently into the cloudless night sky from his chair by the fireplace, a brooding king on the eve of an unforeseen battle.

Chapter Six

A Portrait of the Violinist
as a Young Artist

H olmes was away throughout the day and I had the opportunity to tend to my dwindling medical practice. When our guests and we had reassembled for the evening, Holmes was sombre but relaxed. Miss Delumeau too, I was happy to see, exuded a calmness hitherto not in evidence, which augmented the lustre of her beauty. I now had a glimpse of her own commanding presence as an incipient star in the operatic firmament, a presence for which her exceptional physical beauty was merely a scaffold. Youth and worry had disguised a strength that could no longer be mistaken. Maestro del Nero was fairly bursting with excitement: his rehearsals had no doubt been going quite well.

"It is responding, Mr Holmes, this violin of yours. I think it fancies me!" he chuckled. "It is of course not the *Medici*, but it has its own refreshing personality. You see, Mr Holmes, those who believe that pine and maple die a death when they are cut and shaped and varnished are not correct: wood remains alive, alive and sensitive. It responds to love and withers with neglect. A great musician such as myself who lavishes consistently upon the violin exalted harmonies will change the very structure of its fibres so that it breathes and resonates more freely. A poor one who trades in discord will bring pain and stricture. And if a violin remains untouched and unsounded for too long, it will be dead forever. Like a human child who must be nourished and guided by a loving hand, so is the violin. I tremble to think how near the *Medici* was to becoming a permanent resident of Hades."

The virtuoso sipped delicately from his glass and then rose and moved towards the open windows. "To breathe freely, Mr Holmes ..." The maestro became pensive.

"As a infant I was sickly, having been born a month before my time, though the caul was a consolation to my dear mother who saw in it a sign of greatness. Breathing was an effort and I nearly died before my first year. Everything good and strong within me I owe to that extraordinary woman. My father did not deserve her, believe me. He was a mason who, returning to Florence from Siena, chanced to pass a gypsy camp. There was dancing and music and he and his fellows were invited to join in, no doubt after donating to the cause. My mother and her brothers were playing their fiddles and my father's eye was caught by her beauty, and by the uniqueness of a female musician. He himself, a handsome man in his youth, made an impression.

"He sacrificed a month's earnings for her hand, which her father accepted that very night. Whether he liberated her from a life of wandering, or whether she fled to a protector is not known, but she returned with him to Florence, fiery and impetuous as she was, and brought her fiddle.

"A stationary life with a coarse spouse soon became tedious, but she took refuge in music. My father at first reacted like a savage, for it was unbecoming of an Italian's wife to devote her energies to anything but servitude in the home. But then, as her talent and will could not be suppressed, he turned them to advantage and encouraged her to play in public, outside the Duomo or the Baptistery, in the Piazza della Repubblica, on the bridges over the Arno, and soon she was earning with her gypsy airs and melodies far more than my father with his masonry. He would have become prosperous solely from my mother's earnings had it not been for his drinking. Instead he forsook his craft and spent his days shepherding my mother and keeping watch over the monies and the men whom she attracted by her playing even as she carried me within her.

"He despised me for my sickliness and for the attentions I drew from my mother who doted on me, and for his necessary return to work. But nearly as soon as I could crawl I accompanied my mother on her rounds. It was a joy for me to listen and watch her, and a time of great happiness for, truth be told, her work was not arduous – a few hours and we would be home, and still she would play to amuse me and herself between chores.

"She encouraged my fascination with the fiddle, Mr Holmes, and even now I can recall the scent of her as she held me in her arms and guided my hands on the instrument, which I sought out as soon as she put it aside. What need was there of childish toys when I could endlessly amuse myself with this wondrous source of pleasure? I plucked its strings and moved the weighty bow across them and learned to stop them with my fingers to produce a delightful variety of tones. It was so big in comparison to my small body! My mother's pride knew no bounds when she came upon me and saw that I had positioned it as a cello, between my knees, and struggled to bow and even yet succeeded in creating something pleasing to the ear.

"One day outside the Duomo an elegant elderly gentleman paused to listen to my mother's melodies. I shall never forget it: he was a short man with a most luxuriant white moustache, and my mother was playing a languorous tune when he passed. He reached down into his pockets and withdrew a golden coin, which he gave to me. You see, I held a shawl for donations, and I rushed to sit at my mother's feet while she played. The man folded his bony white hands on the crest of his walking stick and he remained listening intently. After each air he beckoned to me and yet another gold coin would appear. My mother beamed and played for what seemed like ages, whilst my father eyed the growing riches with his customary avarice and vigilance lest they be stolen. A crowd grew around us. The stranger, as the summer evening wore on, doffed his hat and made to approach my by now exhausted mother. He produced a card that identified him as a teacher of music, and he addressed the three of us solemnly: 'I thank God to have introduced me, so late in life, to a true musician'. My mother blushed and curtsied. 'The Signora has an immense talent, but it will stagnate without proper nourishment and training. I have been a humble servant of the art of Orpheus for decades and I have helped many to rise above the mundane. May I play something for you?'

"My parents could scarcely refuse after his generosity thus far, and the gentleman accepted my mother's violin and proceeded to bring forth a music that took my breath away. His aged fingers were nimble and though his tone was rather thin my mother and I were entranced. After returning the violin he addressed my sceptical father directly. 'Signor, may I have the privilege of offering my services to your wife – gratis, of course? If you would be kind enough to escort her to my quarters tomorrow at four, she may decide whether my skills would enable her to enrich and elevate her talents'. He bowed deeply and turned, but my mother ran to him, flustered and eager. 'Thank you, Cavaliere, thank you, but please, kind sir, tell me what music it was you played just then, and is there more of it?' He laughed gently: 'The music of Bach is infinite, Signora. Until tomorrow'.

"Signor Ferruccio Tagliavento changed my mother's and consequently my own life irrevocably. The next day at the appointed time he introduced her to greater glories of Bach and to the discipline of formal training. She of course until then had never read a note of music in her life, but she submitted herself to the rigours of study with delight. And she shared them with me. Somehow the translation of musical notation into sound was second nature to me and my mother was astonished at my facility.

"It was only a short while before Signor Tagliavento, despite his years, made advances to my beautiful mother. He was, after all, an Italian man and her charms were irresistible. I knew something was amiss one afternoon. A boy in love with his mother could not help but understand such things, even if vaguely. She dared not confide in my father who would have beaten her and called an end to her instruction, so she devised a clever solution. She had me accompany her to her lessons. At first Signor Tagliavento was displeased but his love of music transcended his frailties and he generously endured my attendance. I for my part relished the opportunity to enter a secret and magnificent world, quietly witnessing the blossoming of my mother into a genuine artist and greedily taking in all that transpired. One day, as she struggled with a difficult passage, I leapt from my corner and volunteered to play it for her. Signor Tagliavento frowned at first as the aches of his body had already soured his mood that afternoon, but my mother unhesitatingly gave way. When I executed the passage flawlessly, the good teacher reached out to me in astonishment and kissed my forehead. 'You are raising a genius, Signora!' he exclaimed. From that day forward half of each lesson was given over to me. We continued thus for nearly two years and by the age of nine I had surpassed my mother in every musical respect. On my tenth birthday Signor Tagliavento gave me a splendid violin, but I refused his gift, insisting it go instead to my mother, who parted with her own. Secretly I cherished her gypsy fiddle and was convinced that in my hands it surpassed her new acquisition.

"During these *anni mirabiles* the two of us partook of the splendours of Bach, Mozart, Beethoven, Haydn – but principally Bach, the father and mother of all. We played together in the streets, performing duets and seasoning our gypsy programme with excerpts from the masters. Bach we performed with great abandon, but chief of my delights was the time we gave to improvising on classical and folk themes in a way that made as one these separate musical domains, all according to the whim of the moment. Those unpredictable excursions gave me no end of pleasure. Such music, Mr Holmes, such joy, Dr Watson!

"Alas, this paradise would come to an end. I greeted news of my mother's pregnancy with alarm. When she told me of an addition to our family I ran off covered in tears, for my child's mind could not abide an intrusion into our bliss. And then genuine tragedy was to befall: Signor Tagliavento passed away in his sleep. My mother and I mourned his death bitterly, yet we carried on the spirit of his teachings which, in fine, amounted to no more than an introduction to new musical worlds and an encouragement of our adventurous exploration of them. Little did I realise how great a teacher he truly was!

"My mother was already large by the time of his death and in such discomfort she could no longer play in public. I therefore took up the cudgels and upon my slim frame fell the burden of supporting our family as my father's unwavering drunkenness rendered him unfit for work. Yet my dear mother, in the midst of her pain, managed to soothe me daily when I returned and proudly poured my earnings at her feet. She revelled in my serenades to her at home and I had forgiven her betrayal.

"The fateful day arrived, Mr Holmes. My mother's anguished cries told me that yet another tragedy had occurred, one without compare. She perished in childbirth, as did my unborn brother. My world had been utterly destroyed."

Here the great man paused, and in the sombre evening light the pain of his reminiscences was etched upon his brow. But he drew himself up and continued.

"In my frenzy of grief I dashed to pieces our violins. Better nothing than anything! Yet in every catastrophe there may be some good. I soon found myself to be the beneficiary of Signor Tagliavento's Amati violin and much, much more. The good man, having no family, had bequeathed to me a magnificent inheritance, very carefully stipulated. It included the villa in Fiesole that has been my home since coming of age, and a musical education at the Conservatoire.[1] He was a banker, Mr Holmes, who, having made his fortune, could then afford to indulge himself in his true love. The old man, knowing my father, was careful to set aside a fixed amount

---

[1] For reasons of tact I am compelled to conceal the name and location of the institution. (JHW)

for living expenses, strictly and regularly withdrawn by agents of the Conservatoire. So away we went, my father and I, to the city of light and promise.

"To a frightened child it was a dazzling and fearful place. My audition at the Conservatoire was a foregone conclusion. Had I possessed no musical skill whatsoever they would have happily accepted Signor Tagliavento's bequest, but as it was I created a sensation.

"I will spare you the details of an education that strove to extinguish all music within me. They would have me play Bach like a mincing French dancing-master! And because my intonation and dexterity were flawless – this is modesty, Dr Watson, not boastfulness – they focused their criticisms on my interpretative abilities and condemned all exercise of liberty. They told me exactly how to play and they stressed the spectacular effect, an exaggeration of dynamics and tempo. Their cheap tricks filled me with scorn. During my lessons I acquiesced to my instructors' insipid demands, but I was wise enough to nurture my abilities independently. I devoured the violin literature and called upon the spirit of my mother to improvise on gypsy pieces and classical themes for refreshment.

"In the area of technical proficiency what can I tell you except that my mother, Signor Tagliavento and the streets of Florence taught me everything? I learned left-handed pizzicato when I was forced to scoop up wayward coins with my right even as it held the bow. I could secure the violin with my chin so that both hands were freely mobile. In fact, my mother played a game with me. She would fling a coin to my left and I was challenged to catch and pocket it without disturbing the melody I played. It was exceedingly difficult, but I learned well enough to enhance my earnings considerably, for the public delight in such displays.

"The true secret of technique, however, is relaxation. And no better schooling in this can be imagined than provided by the circumstances of my childhood. To play while walking, turning, bowing, speaking, and even dancing – one could not be anything *but* relaxed on the fiddle. And make no mistake:

71

for me the violin was *play*. At the Conservatoire I discovered incredulously that my colleagues had often been beaten and coerced into developing their talents.

"The tension created by my having to maintain a docile facade was, however, too much to bear. My father meanwhile had taken up with a woman who shared his love of indolence and I scarcely saw him. By the age of thirteen I had become a handsome lad who turned precociously to drink and vice and at least in this regard became a model student, for my teachers were experts in these fields. This phase was thankfully short-lived and did not interfere with my debut which was, as you undoubtedly are aware, a 'phenomenon'. But it was undoubtedly also a curse. The pressures to conform had won out. I played not according to my own true self, but to the instructions and expectations of my inferiors.

"I graduated from the Conservatoire with highest honours at the age of seventeen and already an established career. Success bred success but imperceptibly I had come to adopt the very manners and superficialities I had initially loathed. Everywhere I was feted! I could do no wrong! This is not to say that all of my playing was corrupt, but I knew in my heart that the path to greatness was little by little being strangled. I was a blind man making a virtue of darkness.

"You both of you have heard of my exploits, my 'victories' in every major capital of Europe including Prague, where Paganini himself had failed. Everywhere I was in demand, everywhere engaged, my life was a life of ceaseless travel, endless applause, fine food, excellent wine and fawning women ... but I was growing inexorably and inescapably sick. The poison had insidiously infiltrated my very soul.

"So I devised an experiment. You will see, Mr Holmes, what I mean about artists being scientists too. I arranged for a concert in Paris at which I would play the Mendelssohn and Beethoven concerti. Naturally I invited the faculty of the Conservatoire who were only too willing to be associated with their famous pupil. And I set out deliberately to play in a manner antithetical to the great composers' ideas. I exaggerated *everything*: piano became pianissimo, forte fortissimo, presto prestissimo and andante adagio. I created spurious contrasts from phrase to phrase. By turns I smiled beatifically or grimaced with passionate fury. Whenever possible I finished off each phrase with a flourish of the bow, describing an arc high in the air before descending upon the instrument like a wolf on the fold. In short, whatever tasteless I could attempt I did. And the result?"

We waited expectantly as he surveyed us, and then Holmes broke in.

"It was considered your greatest performance," said the detective. "Indeed, the critics acclaimed you as without peer, past or present."

"Precisely, Mr Holmes. My greatest chicanery became my greatest success. At that moment I saw through the vacuity and hollowness and falseness of the rabble, and I decided to rescue myself.

"Like my famous countryman I found myself in a dark wood where the right way had been obscured, but I had no Virgil to guide my path. I called instead upon the shade of my mother as I sought not only to undo the deleterious effects of the Conservatoire and the public, but to attain something beyond, something I had glimpsed only occasionally, but profoundly, of the possibilities of truth and expression.

"There was another danger of the Conservatoire to which I have not yet alluded, and it was that the study of music became wholly detached from the life which music was intended to convey. We students were submerged into a world of symbolic relations, of note to note, harmony to harmony, composition to composition, while the human condition ostensibly concentrated in these symbols became a trifle, an afterthought. Would it shock you to know how few of us read of history or literature, or could relate the material we were forced to master to our own experiences, experiences curtailed and straitened by life amongst the ghostly reflections of crotchets, quavers and semi-quavers?

"I therefore set for myself the goal of learning as much about the world as possible, and of living within it as fully as I could to broaden the palette of my soul. Signor Tagliavento in his wisdom had arranged for me to receive a fixed stipend until I came of age, neither too much nor too little. I learned to use it judiciously as I embarked on my quest.

"I travelled incognito throughout the entire breadth of the Continent, through your own Isles, and even into great Russia. My violin was of course my companion and with it I translated the histories of my wanderings, but for my ears alone.

"My restless and unquenchable spirit discovered many dimensions of love, as well as of treachery, hope, cynicism, gaiety, courage and even desperation. I sought out my mother's people and witnessed their eternal struggle for survival, yet I did not idealise their vulgarity and coarseness. I heard the music of many a roving troupe, and of many a land, and I sampled also the luminaries of the concert stage. I tasted the poetry of the earth and I read widely as well, a habit not encouraged in that institution. The affectations of musical training were vanishing. Then one felicitous day I stumbled upon a method for gaining access to a hidden musical universe. May I describe it?"

The maestro's audience was spellbound; Holmes and I nodded silently in unison.

"It was in the terrible aftermath of a disastrous love affair near Salzburg – Sophie of course knows all – and I was in a most wretched state. To console myself I played feebly a rendition of the duet *Là ci darem la mano* from *Don Giovanni*, and I thankfully soon yielded to exhaustion and fell fast asleep. The scoring of the exchange between Don Giovanni and Zerlina – *Là ci darem la mano, Vorrei e non vorrei* – appeared in a dream with brilliant clarity and the melody was heard richly and distinctly. But then these very notes, the symbols themselves, leapt from the page and joined to form the image of a beautiful woman. The accompanying melody changed concordantly. The phrase was repeated over and over again, and each time a different woman appeared, composed of these musical notes, which sounded out a distinctly new expressive experience – faster, exuberant, delicate, martial, fluid, etc. The variations were endless. The music finally slowed to a dirge and then I saw to my horror the image of my very mother, in all her beauty as I last remembered her alive, every detail, and I could hear within each note a world of colour hitherto unimaginable, though my anguish was unbearable.

"I awoke in a sweat and shook off the shackles of my despair and set off at once for the country of Pushkin and Dostoyevsky. The travels to that great land were long and arduous and I filled my time by putting into the practice the method that had been revealed to me. In the past I had simply picked up my fiddle and glided through a composition bar by bar, my natural musicality and my lightning apprehension of the composer's annotations ensuring a typically engaging result.

"But think, Mr Holmes, and think, Dr Watson, of the score itself! It is a collection of symbols, as we of course know; but what do these symbols represent? They represent in concentrated form the emotional life of the composer, the vast majority of which is unknown even unto himself. His heartache, his joy, his consternation, his piety, his malice, his humour ... his everything to some extent. Yes, he no doubt has wishes as to how to render something within, and he sets these out in musical notation, and he confers a certain form and consciously crafts particular effects; but the great composer is guided by an unknown force and a great work will inevitably express far more than its creator intends.

"One cannot be content with 'playing the music as it is written', or 'strict fidelity to the score' – nonsensical notions at best. The profound interpreter must somehow reach into the limitless reservoir of the unknown and make manifest to the auditor the glories within, behind and around the score: he must tell the composer himself what he does not know.

"I can prove to you both, quite scientifically, that even the slightest of compositions may be rendered in an infinite number of ways. Why, take a measure of four quarter notes. Each note itself may be played in at least a dozen different manners, and I estimate quite conservatively. This one pedestrian bar therefore is capable of no fewer than ..."

Del Nero paused but Holmes leapt into the breach.

"Twenty thousand three hundred and seventy-six variations" he interjected.

"Greater than that," added Sophie, "since you must include variations of phrasing." Holmes nodded thoughtfully in deference.

"Yes, thank you both," continued del Nero. "If you add then a few more measures you have already reached virtually limitless possibilities! Now imagine how richly varied a scope is offered by a Paganini *Capriccio*, let alone a work of true profundity such as a sonata by Bach.

"It also follows therefore that no composer, no matter how illustrious, can rightly be said to be cognisant of the expressive potential of any score. He is aware only roughly of both what he is trying to express and what he has actually succeeded in expressing.

"A musical score is to music heard as a skeleton is to a living human being. We interpreters must breathe life into clay and fashion Woman from a rib. We too are creators of the highest order. I speak not of course of the puppets of our conservatories, but of those valiant souls who have the courage to seek beyond technique and the tissue of falsehoods we call 'tradition'."

"And your method, maestro?" inquired Holmes quietly.

"Ah yes, the method. It is breathtakingly simple: I contemplate. I take a score in hand and either by playing it through or reading, learn it sufficiently to have a sense of its architecture. I then create for myself a meditative repose, an expanse of unshackled time, and allow any thoughts or emotions in response to the music to course through me. I strive to free myself from preconceptions, cultural or historical, or even technical, from censorship of any kind, from each and every constraint upon the imagination. And I repeat this process for nearly every part: phrases, culminating notes, striking harmonic transitions. Like a detective I seek the vast world of meaning behind small clues, and I do not rest until I have apprehended the elusive truths of the composer's imagination which, if there is genius, are infinite in depth.

"Such imagery then infuses my learning and playing, which in turn give rise to additional revelations, and by the time of public performance I have placed my emotional life utterly into the service of artistic expression, and at my most successful an element of spontaneity will carry me unawares to even greater heights.

"During my wanderings through savage Russia, where an extraordinary new music has been emerging, I was inspired to perform in public once again, but on my own terms. In the shadow of the cathedral of Saint Basil in Moscow I decided to assay Bach – not the Bach of my immaturity, but the Bach of my new-found understanding, a Bach without strictures. Within moments a crowd had gathered. These Russians, they are not like you English, Mr Holmes. They live and breathe their passions and music and poetry are as bread to them. I played heedless of the throng, being guided solely by the harmonies of the master into which I delved ever more selflessly. When I had finished there was complete silence. And then the multitude slowly approached, men and women, old and young. I was initially frightened but there was no cause: they paid homage to me as if I were an icon. One after another they pressed my hands to their lips. Thus my genuine career began."

The hour was late. The reverence of which del Nero spoke was palpable and such was its spell that not a word was exchanged upon his exit. He took Miss Delumeau's arm and silently nodded. Holmes and I were left pensive and, curiously enough, without our customary need for tobacco.

Chapter Seven

The Science of the Stradivarii

"Watson," cried Holmes cheerily, "would you fancy an adventure this morning?"

"By all means," I replied, glad for any chance to relieve the tension of unanswered mystery.

"Capital! First the Langham, where the maestro awaits, and then to a small establishment in the vicinity."

Del Nero greeted us warmly and thanked Holmes for the violin, eager to commence practice and rehearsals. Holmes and I strolled from the hotel and after a few minutes turned into New Bond Street. I knew at once our destination: William E. Hill and Sons, Violin-Makers.

"I have just had occasion to reread your excellent monograph on the *Tuscan*," smiled Holmes as we entered the shop. "Watson, may I introduce Mr Alfred Hill, the world's greatest expert, along with his brothers Arthur and Henry, on Cremonese violins, and a superb luthier himself."

"Why, thank you, Mr Holmes," replied Alfred sheepishly, as we shook hands. "And to think that in but a few days' time we will have the opportunity to hear its brother, the *Medici*."

"Are you aware of its history?" asked Holmes, rather cleverly evasive I thought.

"Rumours have reached our ears, Mr Holmes. We understand that it was Paganini's secret treasure, which he bequeathed to an unfortunate lover. How it came into the possession of either Paganini or Signor del Nero is however a mystery. But its authenticity is beyond doubt. I have heard it and indeed in del Nero's hands it has no peer for sheer richness, power, brilliance and variety of tone and shading. Its pianissimo carries to the furthest reaches of a hall with a fullness that is without equal! Only Stradivari himself could have fashioned it. In fact the maestro once promised to let us take its measurements. I can hardly wait for Sunday, when we shall hear it in all its glory."

"Neither can we, Mr Hill. Am I correct, Watson?"

"Quite right, Holmes." I dared not add that we anticipated the event for quite different reasons.

"Now, Mr Hill, if I am not mistaken you and your brothers are nearing completion of your biography of Antonio Stradivari," added Holmes deftly.

"We are nearly there. It has been an arduous undertaking and I fear its audience will be a small one."

"Nonsense, Mr Hill. The edition will sell far faster than you think. You must at all costs reserve a copy for me."

Hill chuckled. "Your contribution to our chapter on Cremonese varnish guarantees you as many copies as you wish."

Holmes bowed slightly in deference to his acknowledgment, then added: "And your work on the master's labels?"

"We have made some very interesting discoveries and will be devoting an entire chapter to them. There has been a great deal of confusion about their importance, but I believe we have amassed much information and clarified matters considerably. In assessing the provenance of an instrument they are virtually indispensable, despite the many forgeries and alterations."

"Splendid. I wonder whether I might inquire about a point or two."

"I trust you are not concerned about your own violin. Its label, though worn, had not been tampered with, I can assure you."

"No, Mr Hill, I have complete confidence in your judgment. However, the matter of Stradivari's habits intrigues my detective mind, as it does yours."

"A true connoisseur! I have many specimens to show you. And what a coincidence – why only yesterday a visitor confessed to an identical interest and I spent the better part of an afternoon describing our work."

"How unusual," muttered Holmes.

"Unusual indeed. Women are seldom so engaged."

"A woman ... and was she slim, of medium height, with dark hair, and did she speak with a slight French accent?" asked Holmes eagerly, adding, "Watson would describe her as rather beautiful, I am sure."

"Beautiful yes, and nearly as tall as you, Mr Holmes, but blonde and German through and through, though her English was excellent. A striking personality."

"Ah," replied Holmes, crestfallen.

"Yes, she demonstrated a remarkable appreciation for the subject of labels and questioned me quite closely about our biography and the conclusions we have reached about Stradivari's work. She was acting on behalf of a collector, but no matter, it was a delight to converse with someone so erudite and passionate about both music and the king of instruments."

At this juncture an elegant and distinguished gentleman appeared from the recesses of the shop. It was no surprise to learn in a round of introductions that this was a brother – Arthur, as it turned out – for the resemblances of facial structure and gait were obvious.

Holmes and Alfred Hill excused themselves to continue their discussions of the labels of Stradivari in private, while Arthur assumed the duties of genial host, offering me a tour of the workshop.

The delicious bouquet of freshly cut maple and pine, the aroma of drying varnish, and the enchanting spectacle of the violin-makers' art on display, modern and antique, delighted and filled me with awe. Arthur Hill, moreover, known for his literary skills and appreciation of history, was my kind of

Englishman: courteous, impeccable in manner, and above all eminently rational. The complexities of the Latin temperament and my lingering concerns about Holmes' methods receded as Arthur patiently described the intricacies of violin construction past and present. The cadences of his mellifluous and quiet voice reaffirmed the native British superiority in matters of science and ratiocination. He spoke proudly of his brother Alfred's growing renown as a maker of bows rivalling Peccatte and Dodd, and concluded our tour by stressing the multiplicity and diversity of factors that accounted not only for the success of the Cremonese luthiers but the creation of any violin of merit.

"You see, Dr Watson," he said as we returned to the storefront, "so many critical variables are in play. The shape and size of the sound-holes, the curvature of the bouts, the thicknesses and arching of the back and belly, the sonority and resilience of the wood, the positioning of the soundpost, the length of the bass bar, the type of varnish and the manner in which it is applied ... why even the purfling affects the sound that is produced! And these may all be perfection itself, yet if the strings are wanting and, more important, if the bridge is not shaped and fitted with greatest precision, all will have been for naught.

"Upon the bridge," he continued, holding an example aloft for me to appreciate, "this slender and much-neglected sliver of wood, depends the functioning of the entire instrument. It must bear all. The horsehair of the bow sets into motion the string, itself made from the intestines of sheep, whose vibration is then transmitted through the bridge and into the body of the violin. Thus the entire instrument begins to vibrate, which vibration causes the ambient air to respond and to produce the glorious sound that caresses our ears. The belly in particular must resonate in such a way that a consistency of tone may be obtained throughout the violin's register. Only pine, by which I mean of course *Abies pectinata* or *Picea excelsa*, possesses such qualities. But it must be chosen and cut with an expert eye. However, the many diverse components of the violin must all function flawlessly together to achieve a desirable result. It is the whole, Dr Watson, the whole, and not one element, no matter how singular, that matters."

"How very like the human body," I mused. "Health may be attained only if each and every organ system is sound. A good heart with a bad brain wouldn't be much use now, would it?"

"Decidedly not, Dr Watson" replied Mr Hill after a curious pause. "Henry and Alfred and I, not to mention our late father, have devoted our lives to the study of the violin. We have possessed many an example of the greatest representatives of the luthier's art, and have taken the most precise measurements. We have even come into possession of Stradivari's formula for varnish ... what, did Mr Holmes not inform you?"

My astonishment was impossible to conceal, for even I had heard stories of the importance of the master's varnish and the pains he took to keep his recipe secret.

"Stradivari's great-great-grandson Giacomo discovered it inside the cover of the luthier's Bible, including instructions for its proper application. He made a copy of the formula but unfortunately destroyed the Bible, ignorant youth that he was. However he refused to reveal it to anyone, not even his wife or daughters. Even as an impecunious volunteer in Garibaldi's campaign, he withstood the temptations of a royal sum. But as he neared the end of his life, he became convinced that only we of all luthiers would uphold the traditions of his famous ancestor and thus did he consent to entrust it. A little wine, I must confess, encouraged his generosity."

"So you have it yourself, the secret varnish?" I asked incredulously.

"Indeed, Dr Watson, but it is not much used: we find our own to be vastly superior. In fact, we have duplicated with unerring exactitude a number of Stradivari's masterpieces, down to every particular detail, including the use of his varnish, and in this manner surpassed even Vuillaume who would have sacrificed an eye for the secret." He paused, pursing his lips pensively.

"And?" I interposed.

"And ... they are good, Dr Watson, quite good, but they do not come close to approximating the merits of the originals – the *Betts*, the *Alard* or the *Tuscan* for example. And do you know why?"

Not realising the question was rhetorical I attempted to respond.

"The age of the wood is my guess."

"Pshaw!" exploded Hill derisively. "There is only one explanation, and believe me, Dr Watson, it has nothing to do with wood."

Hill was fairly glowering at me as if I had committed offence.

"Can you not see, Dr Watson?"

"I'm afraid I don't quite understand," I answered tepidly.

Arthur Hill lowered his voice and glanced round him as if to confirm that we were alone.

"Antonio Stradivari lived into his nineties, and he died a very rich man in Cremona." Hill raised his eyebrows.

"Yes," I murmured uncomprehendingly.

"Surely you realise that to have reached fifty years at the time was a miracle. Why, the man had wives, children, old age, health, riches and immortal fame," he declared impatiently.

"I'm not sure I follow, Mr Hill."

He was visibly flustered and his cheeks reddened as he strove vainly to control himself.

"Are you both blind and deaf?" he hissed.

I was taken aback as Hill advanced upon me barring my route to the door.

"Look at them!" he demanded, indicating the row of antique violins that hung glowing on display, their dazzling varnish catching and refracting the light of the morning. "Is it not strange that sheeps' guts should hale souls out of men's bodies? They stir us with their voluptuous tones, they seduce us into a transient world of inimitable beauty and joy, which becomes a mockery when we are compelled to face the daily toil of our paltry existence. Faust sold his soul, Dr Watson,

Stradivari his instruments. *That,* you fool, is the secret of his violins! They are bedevilled, and their devilry takes possession of those who play upon them!"

He plucked a magnificent example from its station and hurriedly fetched a bow.

"Now, Dr Watson, let us see whether you are here for honest cause, or have been summoned," he challenged ominously.

Hill handed me the implements. During the Afghan campaign I had encountered many cases of mental derangement among soldiers for whom the ardours of battle were incapacitating. Their frantic excitement was best managed by indulgence rather than force. I decided to pursue a similar course with Arthur Hill, all the while praying for Holmes' speedy return.

"What are you waiting for? Play!" commanded Hill peremptorily.

I took up the invaluable instrument, having but the vaguest notion of how to position it properly. Perspiration drenched my brow and as I drew the bow across one of the middle strings it bounced chaotically from the trembling of my right hand, producing a harsh and painful rasp that resembled the squeal of a dying cat.

He impatiently snatched both fiddle and bow and took them up himself. Eyeing me malevolently he kissed the handle of the stick, murmuring, "A prince among bows." He then proceeded to play a kind of Irish jig, loud and furious, while hectically capering about the showroom.

"Arthur!" called Alfred sharply as he and Holmes re-emerged to my grateful relief.

"Yes," his brother responded, deftly replacing the instrument, "I was just informing Dr Watson of the science behind the Stradivarii and he was desirous of a brief demonstration," he continued smoothly.

"Thank you," replied Alfred, levying a minatory glance. "Now if you would be so kind as to return to the workshop, I will see our visitors out."

Arthur bowed and exited, while his brother chuckled uneasily.

"Arthur is quite passionate about the work, Dr Watson, sometimes perhaps too passionate, but he means well, and is a font of knowledge."

I mopped my brow with my handkerchief and gladly welcomed the open air. I was about to apprise Holmes of my startling encounter once we had reached a safe distance from the Hills, but he chose to prattle on about the orthography of the Roman alphabet, his inexplicable enthusiasm for which prevented any interruption. Suddenly Holmes brought our brisk pace to a standstill. He began to laugh – softly at first, then more and more richly until we had begun to attract attention. He resisted my discreet attempts to urge him along and instead waved me away while in the throes of a mirth I can only describe as diabolical.

It was with considerable trepidation that I returned to our lodgings that evening, after having meandered through the streets of London in a determined attempt to free myself from the claims of superstitious dread. The unnerving behaviour of Arthur Hill followed immediately by Holmes', for whom laughter was as rare as a downpour in the Sahara, had rattled me. Musing upon the eccentricities of those whom I knew to own Stradivari's instruments – Paganini, Ysaÿe, Joachim, Sarasate, del Nero, and Holmes himself – a less scientific mind might have found a disturbing corroboration of the luthier's ravings. Certainly Holmes' own peculiarities appeared to have grown since his acquisition of the violin but, I reminded myself, correlation is not causation. And all this talk of devils and enchantment and so forth was of course mere infantilism. Thus reassured though still by no means at ease about del Nero and his stolen instrument, nor by Holmes' incomprehensible antics, I made my way home.

Del Nero was already there and holding forth as I entered.

"You see, Mr Holmes ... ah, good evening, Dr Watson!" he added jovially, "this invention, so simple in its magnificence, of using a bow upon a gut string, changed humankind. And do you know why? It sounded sweet to the ear, like nothing before."

"Except the human voice," interjected Miss Delumeau.

"Yes, you may be right my dear," replied del Nero with some hesitation and reluctance, "but in the family of non-human instruments nothing could compare. The brass and woodwinds of the 16th century were rough and unpleasing. And the human voice, though potentially divine, has not the expressive capacity of the violin. There can be no argument. It is wrongly asserted that the voice is the model to which we instrumentalists must aspire when in fact it is the very opposite. No, the human voice must look to the violin to realise its capacity to create a flowing line, colour and excitement."

"Dear Donato," cried Sophie, "you are mistakenly assuming that the virtues of your own playing define the average! I confess that as a singer I look to your sound as a guide, but I do not look to others. You are the exception, my darling, that proves the rule of the superiority of the voice."

Holmes observed Sophie closely and, it seemed, with a more forgiving eye than before. Del Nero was not obviously accustomed to be contradicted, at least not in matters of music, but he grudgingly gave way.

"Well, if you speak about the average I grant there is an eminent place for the voice, but how can one not be partial to the violin? Its range alone far exceeds that of the most sublime of voices, not to mention its repertoire of effects."

"And yet you may say the same of the pianoforte," interjected Holmes.

"The pianoforte! Please, Mr Holmes, do not insult me. It too has its place – it is a superb supporting instrument, but it is after all an instrument of fixed pitch. Why even Dr Watson can play a fine note on the pianoforte! I use you merely as an example, my good sir," he nodded to me. "But to elicit a beautiful one on the violin, just one note, mind you, is an effort of which few are capable."

The natural vehemence that had crept into del Nero's own voice could not be suppressed and I grew uneasy as our genial gathering a scant two days in advance of the concert threatened to become a battleground. As I later learned it was not unusual for musicians to engage in such internecine conflict, and generally over the smallest of points. It was Sophie Delumeau who brought our attention back to science – not the science of Arthur Hill, thank heavens, but of Helmholtz and Fourier, surprising Holmes to no end.

"So when Donato plays an exquisite note, as only he can, what we hear is a series of pure tones simultaneously. There is a fundamental tone that like the sound from a tuning fork vibrates at one particular frequency alone; it is the slowest of the series, and is responsible for the note's pitch. A number of other pure tones, which we may call 'overtones' or 'harmonics' are present and these vibrate faster, at frequencies that are exact multiples of the fundamental. Except," she added quickly as Holmes stirred himself, "it is far more complex. For these 'overtones' are really never *exact* whole number multiples. They are always varying slightly and even somewhat randomly. Nor is it exclusively the fundamental that determines pitch. Add to this complexity the fact that the ways in which Donato produces a note with the fingers of his left hand and his bowing are infinite, and they all of them contribute to these incessant variations of the harmonics and thus create his characteristic and irreproducible timbre."

Holmes in his eagerness could not be restrained. "Therefore the most minute change in pressure or positioning of either hand, of any finger for that matter, leads inexorably to an alteration of timbre, which itself affects the whole of what he is attempting to convey. And how to account for these fluctuations? Why the influences of his entire life history are at work! All that has shaped him and which he has absorbed will leave their mark on his execution. A simple musical phrase is as telling as a fingerprint."

"And consider also," I added, "the physiological mystery represented by the transformation of something as ethereal, invisible and intangible as a mere thought which, originating in the brain, is somehow converted into an impulse that is then conducted by the nervous system to the peripheral musculature."

"Bravo, Watson: *rem acu tetigisti!*" exlaimed Holmes. "Neither science nor philosophy will manage an answer to that in our lifetimes."

"But do not forget the *Medici*, my dear Sophie! Or Mr Holmes' violin," del Nero added hastily, "for without their contribution ..."

"You would still be without peer," asserted Sophie. Del Nero merely smiled in silence. "Furthermore, Mr Holmes," she continued, "just as there is light that cannot be seen by the human eye, so are there sounds that are beyond the reach of the ear. And as these unseen waves of light have effects on us of which we are not aware, for good and ill, so too with sound. Think of the multiplicity of the tones and overtones that cannot be heard, Mr Holmes, when Donato plays but which must influence us nonetheless in ways we cannot understand. Therein lies his greatness: in a realm that cannot be conventionally grasped by our senses."

Holmes was about to raise an inquiry when Miss Delumeau forestalled him.

"My father was a physicist, Mr Holmes, and he believed that an education in the physical and mathematical sciences should not be denied the fairer sex."

"I have chosen wisely, have I not?" boomed del Nero, rising from his seat and draining his glass of wine.

"Mr Holmes," he continued, "the Lord may have rested on the Sabbath, but del Nero cannot afford to go an entire day without labour. He – rather, I – will confine myself to half a day of practice with your violin. The other half I devote to mental preparation – to my 'creative contemplation'. Tomorrow evening, in anticipation of my concert the following day, I must excuse myself from your company and will have time only to return the instrument to you for safekeeping. I have thoroughly enjoyed our conversations, Mr Holmes, but I must be prepared for an encounter with the gods. *Au revoir*, my friends."

89

"Good luck, maestro," said Holmes. "Watson and I will naturally be at the performance, and afterwards we will gather here to celebrate what will no doubt be a magnificent concert, and," he added, "the restoration of the *Medici*."

I saw our guests to the threshold, bidding them good night. Unexpectedly Miss Delumeau turned towards me as she descended the stairs, her eyes wide and luminous in wordless supplication.

Chapter Eight

Intermezzo

I slept fitfully that evening. Sophie Delumeau's entreaty as she took her leave, unnoticed by the others, had in conjunction with the preceding anomalies of the day enhanced my uneasiness. Sherlock Holmes, having returned from the Langham, greeted me with casual bonhomie. I was therefore emboldened to confront him with my misgivings.

"Patience, my friend" he replied. "We are entering a new age of criminal detection, an age in which the most important question is *why* rather than *how* or *who*."

With this baffling rejoinder he left for the library of the British Museum to initiate fresh researches into the origins of polyphonic music.

"The subject intrigues me to no end," he said with childish excitement. "A full day of scholarship, the concert tomorrow – London does have its virtues."

I did not count among those virtues the fog that had begun to slither its way into our streets, breaking the spell of fine weather we had enjoyed, and accentuating the obscurities of the case of the missing Stradivarius. Try as I might I could not dismiss the oddities and insouciance of my friend's behaviour. It seemed as if under the influence of music and the violin (for thankfully there was not evidence of other influences) his typically keen judgment had been compromised. Accustomed as I was to the unorthodox methods of Sherlock Holmes, which often produced brilliant results, in this instance I confess I had lost confidence, fearing that this particular investigation would, like a number of other cases I have deliberately kept from the public, meet with failure.

There were merely a few reliable facts: the loss of the violin and pearls, and Miss Delumeau's apprehension. The rest was conjecture. Holmes' guarantee of the return of the violin might well be a bluff: it would not be the first time he took liberties with a client. Presumably his intention would be to preserve the maestro's confidence and allow the performance to take place without disturbance. But afterwards?

And what of Miss Delumeau's well-being? From the very beginning Holmes' focus had been on del Nero and the violin – to such an extent that the minutiae of Roman orthography could take precedence over Miss Delumeau's suffering. Though partially explained by Holmes' immunity to feminine allure, it could not be justified. Surely we bore responsibility for any harm that might come to her.

I knew for a fact that Holmes esteemed instinct and intuition in the field of criminal detection, skills which distinguished the outstanding from the mediocre. So too in music. This 'creative contemplation' of which Signor del Nero spoke – was it not similar to what my friend accomplished by those long stretches of enforced solitude during which, coffee and foul shag tobacco at hand, he unravelled the skein of a riddle? The observation and collation of facts alone were not sufficient: it was the ability to see beyond them that characterised excellence.

In medicine my own intuitive apprehension of signs and symptoms had invariably resulted in diagnostic success. I therefore put into practice this very same art with the indisputable facts of our case before me and soon found myself trembling as I came to grips with a realisation that brought the entire affair into a new and most perilous clarity – *Del Nero and his infernal fiddle were mere pawns in a larger drama involving his young and beautiful fiancée!*

I strained to imagine with greater definition the exact nature of the drama which Sherlock Holmes, under the sway of the accursed *Medici*, had utterly overlooked.

And then it dawned upon me: like a bacillus brought into sharp relief under the focus of a microscope, so the answer emerged. In a matter of seconds, my mind had as it were of its own accord recalled del Nero's seduction of Miss Delumeau and the devastation it had visited upon her lover. The unfortunate young man – and of his youth, in contrast to del Nero, there could be no doubt – heartbroken, distraught and then seething with anger, swore revenge. With the theft of the violin he would deal a terrible blow to del Nero, for whom a musical calamity was worse than death – in fact, would have meant a lasting humiliation. But for his former mistress he reserved, in a manner typical of the passionate but cowardly attitude of the Latin male towards the weaker sex, the more definitive and conventional end: murder. There was not a moment to lose, for such a cunning malefactor would choose to execute vengeance with impeccable timing: on the eve of the great event.

I hurriedly donned an overcoat and reached the Langham in short order, hoping desperately that I had stolen a march on our evil foe. The lobby was crowded and I impatiently pushed my way through the heedless masses and bounded up the palatial staircase. Breathlessly I turned in the direction of Miss Delumeau's suite.

The words '*morto, morto*' and 'Mario', followed by a high-pitched and plaintive scream in which the sadness and terror of a thousand souls might have been expressed, pierced my heart, for they told me my fears had been confirmed. She was dying!

Fighting through despondency made even keener when I realised that in my accursed haste I had neglected to take my revolver, I threw myself against her door with every ounce of strength. If I could not save the wretched Sophie Delumeau, I might yet hope to apprehend the Italian villain, that despicable and murderous cur Mario. Bursting into the suite I saw Miss Delumeau on her knees, a look of bewildered fright on that ravishing face. And then I saw nothing at all.

* * * * *

"Easy, my friend," soothed a familiar voice. My head was throbbing with pain and my vision so blurred I could hardly make out the features of Sherlock Holmes above me. There was another voice, lighter and comforting. Could it be that I had succeeded after all! It was without doubt Sophie Delumeau's, though my condition was such that I could only with difficulty direct my gaze to confirm the impressions of my ear. She pressed a cool cloth against my brow and a soft pack of ice to the right side of my head. I made as if to speak but a sensation of such vast relief and calm overtook me so entirely that I fell fast and joyously asleep.

I awoke on the Sunday, having slept for nearly twenty hours. My head was sore but I was refreshed – *mens sana in corpore sano* once again.

I shall never be more grateful to Sherlock Holmes than for the treatment he conferred upon me that morning. So easily might he have scoffed, gloated or belittled, condescended, patronised or derided. Instead, with the utmost gentleness and compassion, proving beyond all measure the depth of our friendship, he patiently and kindly explained the outcome of my heroic but misguided quest.

While Signor del Nero was rehearsing in the Music Room of the Langham with his accompanist, Sophie Delumeau undertook to run through a particularly challenging and climactic scene from a relatively new Italian opera in which she was engaged to appear. The scene in question, at the very end of the work (whose title escapes me), demands from the singer utmost veracity, and she took the opportunity of the maestro's absence to practice over and over the pertinent passages, which concerned the death of the heroine's lover by firing squad. My boisterous and admittedly impetuous entry into the Langham had excited the attention of one of the private detectives Burleigh kept on hand whenever distinguished guests were accommodated. The man watched and followed me closely, and assuming by appearances that I had intended to visit harm upon Miss Delumeau, knocked me unconscious with a cosh. Burleigh handled the misunderstanding with his customary discretion and managed to transport me back to Baker Street without arousing the notice of his clientele. Miss Delumeau insisted on accompanying me to provide succour; and she also discovered, in the person of the hotel detective, the man who had passed her on the stairs the night of her arrival.

"Well," I ruefully admitted to Holmes, "at least one mystery has been solved."

"That's the spirit, my dear fellow. Now please allow me to recommend a morning of quiet and repose, the better to prepare for the delights that await us."

I smiled warmly in acquiescence and spent the hours before the concert musing upon the inscrutability of human motivation as Holmes strutted and fretted within and without our lodgings in excited anticipation of a long-awaited denouement.

Chapter Nine

The Food of Love

The great Queen's Hall was crowded a full hour before the scheduled start of the concert. A gleaming and magisterial Erard grand piano graced the otherwise empty stage. Holmes had insisted on arriving early and amused himself by roving about the audience with his opera glasses. For violin performances Holmes invariably selected seats near the rear of the hall, as this gave the truest acoustical measure of the instrument's capabilities. As predicted all of musical London – and many from the Continent – were in attendance.

"There, Watson," he exclaimed, "that young fiddler – mark him, for his star is on the rise. Interestingly enough he plays only with the middle section of the bow, but with an expressive charm as befits a Viennese. I hear he is about to tour America. And look – the Czech – no, the youth with that great mane of hair. A brilliant technician, some say greater than both Paganini and del Nero in pure virtuosity, though wanting as a musician. But the others have not yet arrived. Wait, there is someone you may recognise."

He handed me the glasses and I observed with consternation that Arthur Hill was gazing in our direction while his brothers chatted. I frowned and quickly turned away, to Holmes' amusement.

The din of nearly three thousand eagerly expectant music-lovers grew louder by degrees as the hour of reckoning approached. Then suddenly a buzz – followed by a short burst of applause as a small man with bushy grey hair and a black moustache strode to his place in the front row.

"Pablo de Sarasate," murmured Holmes. "What a tone! But he lacks depth I am afraid. And the moustache is dyed. Ah, Watson, there he is, the Belgian! He has grown as wide as his vibrato!" Another burst of applause as the robust and venerable Ysaÿe took his seat also in the front row.

Holmes was obviously enjoying himself – why should he not? The cherished dream of hearing his beloved Stradivarius in the hands of an expert for a programme that would try its mettle to the utmost was about to be fulfilled. And afterwards Holmes would be giving his own performance, with expectations just as keen and an outcome of lasting import. I wondered where the culprit who perversely held the *Medici* hostage might be found among us.

Sophie Delumeau had by now appeared and occupied a box alone, queenly in composure. Not far from her sat Sir Charles and Lady Hallé. Holmes however seemed restive until at last an elderly gentleman entered, wizened and heavily bearded, and the audience erupted in acclaim.

"Joseph Joachim," he nudged, "the friend of Mendelssohn, Liszt, Clara Schumann, Brahms, a true master. And look – he is already quarrelling with Sarasate! I might have known … the Spaniard is a trickster and must have deliberately taken Joachim's seat, and now they must exchange places."

Holmes shook his head and described for me how Sarasate titillated his audiences by appearing to let his Stradivarius fall before catching it up by the scroll at the very last instant.

"An inveterate showman," chuckled Holmes.

Suddenly from behind us came an emphatic "Hush!". I turned to see who the curmudgeon might be and was surprised to find a man younger than I expected, lean, fiendishly bewhiskered and sharp-eyed, who regarded us with reproach.

"Corno di Bassetto has returned from the grave," whispered Holmes, before an even more stentorian "SSSSHHHH!" ensued. To avoid further unpleasantness I decided to study the programme, which read as follows:

QUEEN'S HALL, LANGHAM PLACE

RECITAL CONCERT

SUNDAY, 27 OCTOBER, 1901, AT 2.15 P.M.

==

PROGRAMME

Mozart: *Violin Concerto No. 4, D Major* (piano reduction)

Beethoven: *Sonata for Violin and Piano, No. 9, A Major*

Schubert: *Valse-Caprice No. 6*

Bach: *Partita for Solo Violin, E Major*

Del Nero: *Zingaresque*

DONATO DEL NERO, Violin

with pianoforte accompaniment

The audience is politely requested to refrain from applause

before, during and after the performances

A very tall man in formal wear entered and crossed the stage to take up his post by the piano. His hands were immense and his face marked by an indescribable sadness, as if he had been subjected to some terrible personal tragedy and had not yet recovered. The Russian stood deferentially while the lights dimmed and the clamour of the hall diminished as if the audience had just taken and held its collective breath.

Then del Nero appeared. I nearly burst into laughter when I first espied him, but the fear of censure from Mr di Bassetto kept me in check. He was wearing a garment that seemed a combination of Greek chlamys, Roman toga and ecclesiastical cassock. It was collarless and black, falling skirt-like nearly to the floor, but leaving del Nero's left shoulder and arm completely bare. He resembled a schoolboy's costume-party version of a Druid priest.

Del Nero walked slowly from the wings of the stage to the centre. Applause could not be contained, which caused him to interrupt his progress and glare out at the spectators until they quieted. This happened several times before he reached his destination. Joachim, Sarasate and Ysaÿe were exchanging glances, having obviously realised that del Nero was without his talisman, the *Medici*. Was one among them the villain, or had they conspired together? The mystery was too much so I decided simply to surrender to the moment and enjoy what I could.

The lugubrious Russian sounded an 'A' on the Erard, and del Nero took barely a second to ensure that Holmes' violin was completely in tune. Then the great man gracefully raised his bow and began to play. Was this Mozart? A general rumbling ensued, but Holmes smiled broadly and the audience sighed in unison with relief when they eventually recognised the strains of *God Save the Queen*, the virtuoso's homage to the monarch we still mourned.

Never has the failing of language been more evident to me than in this my feeble and doomed effort to describe the experience of that afternoon, the visual world being far easier for our words to convey than the world of sound. I will nonetheless offer these untutored impressions of del Nero's achievement, all the while begging the reader's forgiving indulgence.

I heard not a violinist that day, but music. Del Nero the man was as one with his instrument as a Cossack his horse, and inconspicuous in the service of the visions he translated for our ears. There was posturing neither of face nor of body. His motions were as supple and graceful as a sapling stirred by the gentlest of winds. But the sonorities that came forth!

Was ever Mozart rendered with more grace, fluidity and richness, or Beethoven with greater muscular sagacity? Schubert's waltz was executed with such robust freedom and abandon that I feared that Bach would be anticlimactic – but not so! With the E major partita the maestro, 'quiring to the young-eyed cherubins', brought us into the realms of the celestial. It was no prettified Bach however, but Bach in rough joyful glory and fierce exuberance. The audience, heedless of the programme's warning, and unable any longer to restrain their pent delight, leapt to their feet at the conclusion of the partita and the aged Joachim gave his imprimatur. He approached the foot of the stage, hands above head to lead the rhapsodic applause. "*Viva L'Imperatore!*" sounded deafeningly from a claque of vociferous Italians to our left.

Holmes was ecstatic. Any doubt about the quality and capability of his fiddle had conclusively been laid to rest. I could hardly imagine even the fabled *Medici* surpassing it, to be frank.

Yet there was more to come!

None knew what to expect from the final piece, this *Zingaresque*. Del Nero allowed some time for the din to subside, his countenance having softened to show greater tolerance for the foibles of his appreciative brethren. And when he again took up the bow he created what Holmes later advised might be an entirely novel musical genre. Yes, it had gypsy influences, as its title suggested, but it transcended the narrow parameters of that folk idiom to suggest the irrepressibly sublime, the unpredictable, and the demonic glee of levitation. Even the pianist showed signs of gaiety and liveliness, as with a now unclouded brow he engaged in answering and further stimulating del Nero's excursions. And just when we thought there could be no greater resolution of his harmonic progressions, a shift in the feeling-tone of the music carried us into yet another direction.

I had lost all track of time as I marvelled and revelled in these unexpected pleasures. Ysaÿe swayed rhythmically from side to side, Sarasate bobbed his head, and Joachim shook his wrist as if he himself were bowing. From behind us di Bassetto tapped his foot. It was impossible for any to remain unmoved – or unmoving. Yet a glance at Sophie Delumeau was most telling of all, for even from a distance I could see that she exuded love, a love that radiated palpably from her to del Nero and from del Nero to us and back again, and all around.

The magnificent violinist ended with the softest of colourful whispers, a ravishing pianissimo that evoked that breath upon a bank of violets of which our dearest Shakespeare wrote. He insisted on bringing his reserved accompanist forward to share in the rapturous reception, but the man soon slid surreptitiously away, and each time del Nero attempted to make an exit the roaring applause swelled like a wave, halting his progress. Drenched and glowing, the maestro bade his adieu with a deep bow, and during the brief lull that ensued a lone stentorian voice from the gallery pierced the hall: "Del Nero *non ripete!*" Del Nero chuckled, levelled his bow at the audacious and witty admirer, and finally disappeared.

Holmes seized me by the arm and we recklessly sliced our way backstage through the adoring throng, overtaking the equally determined di Bassetto to my delight. The maestro beckoned us to the privacy of his dressing-room, past tables laden with food and champagne thoughtfully prepared for his grateful public. I bowed to Miss Delumeau, who answered with the sweetest of smiles, while my friend gave me the shock of a lifetime when without warning he seized del Nero and planted a kiss on each of his fleshy cheeks.

"Until eight tonight!" he reminded the startled musician.

As we stepped outside into the cool afternoon air of the earthly world, leaving the maestro to his ecstatic admirers, not even the baleful eye of Mr Corno di Bassetto could perturb our deep contentedness.

"Pay him no mind, Watson," counselled Holmes, "he is not only a critic but a vegetarian as well, and thus in chronic ill-humour."

Chapter Ten

Voilà

At eight o'clock sharp Signor Donato del Nero and his fiancée Mademoiselle Sophie Delumeau appeared at our door.

"Mr Holmes! Dr Watson!" exclaimed the violinist. "To get away in time ... I thought perhaps it would not be possible. Such a crowd!"

"Pray, accommodate yourselves," greeted Holmes.

While the maestro in the aftermath of his extraordinary performance was ebullient, Miss Delumeau seemed to have reverted to the nervousness and worry of our early acquaintance.

"I must say, Mr Holmes, I may have done Joachim a disservice. He is after all a fine chamber musician. And even Sarasate and Ysaÿe have their merits. We four had quite a discussion. Apparently my little *Zingaresque* made an impression upon them, as it did on that bearded fellow who cornered my poor Russian. They wanted the score. 'The score?', I replied, 'the score is here!'" Del Nero held a finger to his temple.

"I told them it was high time that invention returned to our music. Mozart, Beethoven, Bach – they were all of them improvisers. As for Sergei, he came alive, did he not? It has been an effort for him merely to appear before the public. He prefers anonymity for the moment and forbade me even to acknowledge him on the programme. But that unpleasant man accosted him, harping incessantly on the symphony he refuses to publish after the debacle in St. Petersburg some years ago, for which incidentally the drunken Glazunov was wholly to blame. A most unpleasant display of English manners, I am afraid to say. And there was more to come from him: he is some kind of socialist and was keen to ply Sergei about the condition of the Russian peasantry. Can you imagine!

"Don't you mean the Italian, Mr di Bassetto?" I asked.

"Please, Dr Watson, he is no more an Italian than I am an Englishman," replied del Nero.

"An old pseudonym, Watson," added Holmes, "in use during the days when he was a critic of musical performance in London, a lively and informative one, though strongly opinionated. He has now taken to preaching in other ways."

"Well, Sergei managed to slip away at last. I hope not to the comforts of vodka again. In any case, Mr Holmes, my colleagues were naturally curious about the *Medici* which ..." Del Nero paused expectantly.

"In due time, maestro. It will be here shortly," said Holmes.

"Ah, thank you, Mr Holmes. Such a weight has been lifted. But you know, with this fiddle of yours ... dare I say it? It allowed me to scale Parnassus. The *eletricismo* so valued by Paganini, it was there today, I could feel it! I did not think it would be possible. Now only imagine if I had had my *Medici*!"

Sophie glanced queerly at him as Holmes accepted the Stradivarius with a bow.

"The pleasure has been all mine, maestro. A rare and great privilege."

"But tell me, sir" I interrupted, "is there a reason why your arm was bare?"

Del Nero smiled at Sophie and took her hand.

"How does an Englishman shake hands, Dr Watson, with or without gloves?"

"A gentleman would invariably remove his glove, naturally," I replied.

"So why should I interpose a layer of clothing between myself and my violin? It is essential, Dr Watson, to have the most direct and intimate contact with the instrument. The quality of its vibrations as I bow, which I not only hear but feel in my very bones, will tell me whether I am achieving the desired musical effect, which I may then adjust with much greater accuracy."

"Deucedly ingenious, maestro," I responded, as his argument appealed strongly to my knowledge of the dictates of anatomy and physiology.

"Ingenious indeed," echoed Holmes, the formality of announcement in his voice. He stood with his back to Baker Street and drew himself up to full height. We were being summoned to attention.

"Ingenuity is what brought us all together in the first place: the ingenuity of a thief," intoned the detective. A tension filled the room immediately: the hour had arrived for Holmes' turn on the stage.

"This ingenious thief, however, made the mistake of daring to cross swords with Sherlock Holmes. Not since my skirmishes with the deceased Professor Moriarty have I had so worthy an opponent. I tip my hat to her."

"The German!" I shouted, electrified. "The woman who visited Alfred Hill!"

"Yes, Watson, the woman who visited Alfred Hill: tall, blonde, and whose English was impeccable though her accent Teutonic. Except that she is as German as di Bassetto is Italian, or Signor del Nero English."

"You are quite the showman, Mr Holmes," said Sophie Delumeau, steel in her voice. "Why not get to the point? Have you, or have you not, recovered Donato's violin?"

"I beg your patience, Mademoiselle."

"Male or female, a thief is a thief, Mr Holmes," said del Nero.

"Quite right, maestro." Holmes' lips were pressed tightly together and the mood of the evening began to grow sinister.

"What if I told you, maestro, that the thief is at your side?" continued Holmes, indicating Miss Delumeau.

107

"My good man," I hastened to respond.

Sophie Delumeau rose. "I refuse to subject myself any further to your rudeness."

Del Nero, frantic with confusion, appealed to my friend. I too was bewildered.

"Surely you are joking, Mr Holmes. Yes, of course, it is a joke my dear Sophie. You see, he is like Sarasate. Very good, Mr Holmes, very good," del Nero chuckled, unconvincingly. If indeed this was Holmes' idea of a jest, his timing was execrable. But Holmes' stubborn and enduring silence suggested otherwise.

"Please be seated, Miss Delumeau, and hear me out, all of you. And I am afraid, maestro, you will have to indulge me if you wish to see your precious *Medici* again."

The detective brazenly lit his pipe, though I discerned a minutely tremulous hand. At his tacit signal I opened a window and returned to my seat. Holmes settled into his armchair while the flustered virtuoso struggled visibly. Fearing that del Nero might re-enter a state of emotional paralysis as when we first encountered him, I rushed to his side with brandy. This time he gladly quaffed of the strengthening liquor.

"Discovering that the wily Miss Delumeau stole the *Medici* was a simple thing, as I hope to show you. But why she did it is another matter altogether, and it has the greatest bearing on our inquiry – and your future, maestro.

"You overplayed your hand, Miss Delumeau, from the start. Mistaking Watson for me, and then feigning sudden weakness so dramatically while here – this put me on the alert immediately. But I grant you that the performance in the hackney was of higher quality. You adjusted your behaviour, like any good actress, to your audience's response. The cool poise with which you introduced the 'theft' of the pearls, and the manner in which you cast suspicion, as if by afterthought, on the 'sinister' man who passed you on the stairs of the Langham ... you were positively masterful, Mademoiselle, and nearly had me off the trail, though not for long.

"If you remember, maestro, after Watson's forceful and effective treatment of your stupor, I managed to inspect your violin's case. It was not what I saw that aroused my attention, but what I scented: a hint of lavender. Surely you are not the kind of man to encase your fiddle in something perfumed.

"I carried on with my inspection of your quarters expecting to discover nothing further of import. But I was most eager to examine Miss Delumeau's suite. Sure enough the faint but unmistakeable bouquet of lavender emanating from her dresser could not be ignored. Though for form's sake I continued my investigations, I had already established my hypothesis and it became urgent to test its veracity immediately. Naturally I could not have been so ungentlemanly as to have rummaged through a drawer full of ladies' undergarments. And even if I had recovered the *Medici* on the spot, as I was sorely tempted to do by the prospects of a quick and dramatic success, I would have failed to expose the thief and her motivations. She would have claimed it to be the work of someone else and you, grateful to have had your instrument restored, would have pursued the matter no further.

"And then? Then we would have won the battle but lost the war, for the driving force behind the theft would have remained intact, searching only for a more appropriate opportunity in future. So I devised a solution. I knew that I must keep Miss Delumeau away from her rooms at all costs to prevent her from either destroying – yes, why should I not consider that possibility? – or replacing the violin. Which is why I insisted on our returning *en masse* to Baker Street at once. Maestro, you will recall that Miss Delumeau was reluctant, and agreed only at your persuasive insistence."

Del Nero nodded, wide-eyed, and poured more brandy for himself.

"Watson, my friend, you were right to question my feeble explanation of the crime, that the pearls were the thief's chief aim and that the violin was an afterthought. On the spur of the moment it was the best I could do, but it served at least to distract attention from the *Medici*. The necklace, Miss

Delumeau, was an elegant touch, by the way. I simply grafted my own absurd theory onto your absurd falsehood.

"The sole intention of our journeying here that morning was to ensure that the *Medici* would be retrieved unharmed and kept safe. I had deliberately left my magnifying glass in your suite, maestro, which provided the pretext for our dear Mrs Hudson to fetch it. And I had already arranged with Burleigh to allow her entrance into Miss Delumeau's rooms, which was the actual purpose of her visit. Watson, would you be so kind as to summon the good Mrs Hudson?"

She entered modestly, her hands working away restlessly at the fringes of her apron.

"Now, Mrs Hudson, can you confirm that you retrieved a violin from Miss Delumeau's suite at the Langham Hotel?"

"Why yes, Mr Holmes, a peculiar place to store a fiddle, I thought, amidst a woman's intimate bits and pieces of clothing, but then again, as you have often said, music people are a strange lot."

"Thank you, Mrs Hudson, although I most probably used the word 'musicians'. That will be all."

She curtsied politely and took her leave as unobtrusively as a drifting leaf. The expression on del Nero's face, with its inherited malleability of Italian and Gypsy blood, oscillated between feral rage and mortifying grief. He stared at Sophie with scornful contempt and tearful reproach by turns, and at Holmes with incipient savagery.

"So you, you, you!" he cried to Sophie, "you stole it? And you," turning to Holmes, "you had it all along?"

"Donato, I can explain," entreated Miss Delumeau.

"No!" he railed, "there can be no explanation!"

"Yes there can," added Holmes, "but it is I who will do the explaining. Watson, refill his glass."

Holmes used the interlude to replenish his pipe, but with a sweeter and less offensive tobacco than the shag he so enjoyed – a compromise for the overburdened del Nero no doubt – and I longed for one of our rich Cuban cigars as my own head was spinning with my nerves in an uproar. The mercurial del Nero subsided quickly into a heavy stillness, but he was alert. Miss Delumeau grew calmer and more forceful in presence even though she was silent.

"Yes, maestro," continued Holmes, "the *Medici* was here all along. I had no choice, and judging by the concert today, it did no harm. In fact, the magnificent artistry displayed on another violin, albeit an excellent one, enhanced your stature. For no doubt your peers had been gossiping about the *Medici*'s supernatural qualities and how they alone accounted for your extraordinary artistry. But you proved to yourself, did you not, that you could achieve something without it?"

Del Nero scowled but grunted in assent.

"I repeat: I had no choice, maestro, because without having retained it I would never divine your fiancée's true intentions. You know of Antonia Bianchi, do you not?"

"That consort of Paganini," he replied with contempt.

"Indeed. A singer too, like Miss Delumeau. A singer who loved her middling art more than both the man she lived with and the son she bore him, and who benefited quite handsomely from the notoriety and entrée she received as the partner of the greatest instrumentalist alive. A woman, incidentally, who was not above demolishing her lover's instruments when a fit of rage was upon her."

Sophie Delumeau looked daggers at my friend, but Sherlock Holmes was unassailable. He rose.

"Allow me to reconstruct the crime. You both of you arrived at the Langham: that is fact. But what you did not divulge, Miss Delumeau – nor you, for that matter, maestro – is that you spent the night together. For propriety's sake you engaged two separate suites, as you are not yet married, but after a long and tiresome journey, how likely would it have been for you to stay apart? Remember, you yourself volunteered the information about Signor del Nero's sleeping habits – how he kept the *Medici* well within reach on the right-hand side of the bed.

"You, Miss Delumeau, awoke quite early, and saw your chance. There was the *Medici*! Were you envious of its properties? Did you wish to destroy the career that dwarfed your own? Or were you more innocently curious, burning

111

with a desire to see and touch intimately an object on which the maestro lavished more attention than on you? Signor del Nero, a man of regular habits, would not awaken for at least another hour. The priceless violin, upon which he set so much store, was within your grasp at last. You might never have such an opportunity again."

"And what of the opportunity for me to speak, Mr Holmes?" asked Sophie with cool determination.

"Soon, Mademoiselle, you will have your moment. But for now," he continued undeterred, "let us leave the question of motive aside. You opened the case, removed the violin, and then took the precaution of quietly closing and leaving it, so that if the maestro awoke earlier than expected he would see nothing amiss. You then rushed to the sanctuary of your suite where you could examine the *Medici* undisturbed. How long was it with you ... thirty minutes perhaps? I imagine your contemplating the instrument, stroking it, musing about its wondrous powers, attempting to uncover a secret or two. But unfortunately the maestro rose earlier than expected and immediately sought out his treasure.

"What to do? Had you rushed back and returned it, you would have incurred his unforgiving wrath; it would have meant the end of your engagement, I hazard. Am I correct, maestro?"

Del Nero nodded. "Yes, Mr Holmes. I was very particular about the *Medici* and let no one touch it, not even ..." He could not bring himself to utter his fiancée's name.

"But you are nothing if not ingenious, Miss Delumeau," resumed Holmes. "Hurriedly you devised the story of the second theft. Well done! And you stored the fiddle in the closest and best place at hand, where no one would dare to look. A correspondent of mine in Vienna would find a rich symbolism in your choice."

"Is this true?" croaked del Nero, turning to Miss Delumeau.

"Yes, Donato, it is true, and if I did not know better I would think that Mr Holmes had been there to see it all in person."

Del Nero was crushed and sank further into his seat, bowing his head. Holmes inclined his own as an acknowledgment of the compliment.

"So, maestro, the task I set myself was to discover your fiancée's intent – the *why*.

Her behaviour did not inspire confidence. She is an exceedingly charming woman and it was all I could do to preserve my objectivity. Watson, on the other hand ..." Holmes grinned slyly in my direction.

"The first thing she did, after you returned to the Langham from our rooms was to check that the violin was secure. She discovered, no doubt to her overwhelming dismay, that it was missing, and was thrown into a genuine panic. Naturally she suspected me, in part because I had given facile assurances of its return, though how anyone could believe such a tale is beyond me. Watson was right in calling attention to the gaps in my scenario. You, maestro, on the other hand, swallowed it whole: it is what you wished to believe. Naiveté in an artist may be a virtue, for it is nothing more than a willingness to accept the illogical, the natural domain of art. For a mathematician or physicist, however, naiveté is not so desirable a quality.

"Miss Delumeau is too much the scientist, so the very next day she arranged to pay a visit with the intention of sounding me out and taking my measure. Failing to glean anything of value, she lured my colleague away hoping to prise something out of him beyond my sphere of influence. Your glove, Miss Delumeau, so cunningly laid as bait ... I confess to have overlooked it in my eagerness. As Watson will confirm, even Homer nods. He, however, good and most observant fellow that he is, especially where members of the opposite sex are concerned, snapped at it but could offer nothing more than chivalry. The story of Paganini and Helene von Dobeneck, the manifest reason for her visit, was delivered with consummate skill. Most touching, Miss Delumeau.

"There was nothing for me but to wait, therefore I took care to insist on our evening talks as the only means of gaining insight into Miss Delumeau's actions. When did you realise the *Medici* was in my possession, Mademoiselle?"

"When I discovered that you had visited the Langham that morning, ostensibly to purchase cigars."

"Yes, a rather stupid move on my part. I thought that an unobtrusive observation might tell me something about you, but I had not counted on Watson's agency. A *faux pas* to be sure, which only put you further on your guard and earned me a bruise. But fortunately not a fatal one, for as long as I had the *Medici* you were helpless.

"Signor del Nero, you advocate the 'creative contemplation' of a score. I employ a similar methodology in approaching a conundrum relying, however, unlike you, on a great deal of coffee and tobacco. There now, I am finished. You may breathe more freely."

Holmes relinquished his pipe and rose, pacing across the room.

"During our evening soirees I was handicapped, out of deference to your wishes, but I still succeeded in listening – how shall I put it? – listening with a third ear, if I may coin a phrase. And it was you who provided me with the key to it all."

Del Nero having regained his colour regarded Sherlock Holmes with malevolent curiosity.

"The acquisition of the *Medici*, maestro ..."

"I have told you the unvarnished truth, Mr Holmes, every word!" declared del Nero.

"I do not doubt it, maestro, but it was as unsettling to my mind as a 'wolf' tone to the ear. And eventually it led me to a re-evaluation of Miss Delumeau's character."

"What now," cried del Nero, "has the Lord in his wisdom made you a Solomon?"

"In this instance, yes," responded Holmes suavely.

"Donato," implored Sophie.

"Please do not speak to me!" the maestro replied, covering his ears. Holmes waited for the violinist to recover from the fit of pique.

"The *coup de grace* came during my visit to the Hill brothers. A stroke of genius on both our parts, Miss Delumeau, for we each had arrived independently at a similar conclusion and wished to confirm our theories. You do have flair, Mademoiselle: tall, blonde, Germanic! I was very nearly duped. As Watson will corroborate, the realisation of your trickery struck me forcefully. I laughed like the devil in the middle of New Bond Street, much to my friend's consternation. It is rather easy for a person in disguise to *add* height; but to take it away, as I have had occasion to do, is a taxing ordeal involving contortion and considerable discomfort. A wig and a new accent were of course child's play. You see, maestro, your Sophie is as much interested in the science of the Stradivarii as you or I, and for a very good reason. This venture to England, this concert, maestro ... what possessed you to undertake it?"

"As I said to you before, Mr Holmes, I wished to settle the matter of my place in the rank of instrumentalists once and for all."

"Really?" replied Holmes with sarcastic incredulity. "And all those years, those meanderings through Europe and beyond, those unconventional impromptu performances devoid of pomp, all the time you shunned the established order of the world of serious music, were you concerned about your superiority? Or were you concerned about art, about the greatest and most honest achievement of the human spirit?"

Del Nero blushed deeply, like a chastened schoolboy.

"And after your betrothal not long ago, following a long series of, shall we say, impermanent romantic liaisons, did you not begin to perform more frequently than usual? Think for a moment."

Del Nero stirred and cleared his throat.

"Why, yes, a bit more perhaps."

"Nearly daily, Mr Holmes," added Sophie. "In addition to his practice."

"And did your relationship to the *Medici*, did it perhaps intensify? Did you fret about it, worry about its condition,

115

ruminate on its possible damage or loss, and keep it even more closely at your side?"

"Yes, Mr Holmes," asserted Miss Delumeau. "I can vouch for that. He feared that any perturbation of the *Medici* would affect his ability. He refused to touch another instrument, and he refused to let his own be touched by anyone else."

"Thank you, Miss Delumeau, just as I surmised."

Del Nero sat sullen and restive, unable to speak.

"Now, Watson, please ask Mrs Hudson to bring us the *Medici*."

I did as requested and Mrs Hudson returned with a neatly folded bundle before her. She laid it carefully on our table and noiselessly withdrew.

"Maestro," requested Holmes earnestly, "May I?"

Del Nero tacitly acquiesced. Sherlock Holmes unfurled its velvet sheath to reveal the peerless object. The *Medici* was indeed magnificent: darker than Holmes' Stradivarius, slightly larger, and better preserved. Holmes gently lifted it and turned it over. Something rattled inside and with a delicate shuffle a small string of pearls slipped out of a sound-hole and into the detective's palm.

"Your necklace, Miss Delumeau. An excellent hiding-place providing a beautiful symmetry."

"Now, if I may have my violin, Mr Holmes, I will take my leave of all of you accursed and despicable people."

"You may certainly have your violin, maestro, but first there is something more you must know. Miss Delumeau will do the honours. Come, Mademoiselle, you must be truthful. Dr Watson will be glad to provide assistance."

Sophie Delumeau remained in her chair but spoke with authority.

"Dr Watson, please lay Mr Holmes' violin on the table as well. Thank you. Now would you please copy, exactly as it appears, the lettering on each of the labels within the violins?"

Within a few moments I had rendered the inscriptions visible through the left-sided sound-hole of both fiddles as accurately as I could. Except for the years – the *Medici* showed '1690', and Holmes' '1729' – they were identical:

> ## Antonius Stradivarius Cremonenſis
> ## Faciebat Anno 1690 🅐

and

> ## Antonius Stradivarius Cremonenſis
> ## Faciebat Anno 1729 🅐

"Would you please confirm, maestro?" requested Holmes. Del Nero did so grudgingly.

"Yes, Dr Watson is correct. And what of it? Of course they should be identical. They are the handiwork of Antonio Stradivari."

"There's the rub, Donato!" cried Sophie. "The *Medici* is not a Stradivarius – it is a copy."

"What do you mean, are you all mad?" bellowed del Nero. "It is impossible! My ears do not deceive me, nor my eyes!"

"She is correct, maestro. In 1729 for reasons unknown the great luthier began to employ the Roman 'v' for his surname on the labels. Before that it invariably appeared in what is a semi-cursive form, resembling a 'u'." Holmes wrote it out for him quickly:

> ## Stradiuarius

"The Hill brothers will corroborate this, as they are preparing a biography of Stradivari and have shown me, and Miss Delumeau in disguise, their data, undeniable evidence resulting from painstaking research. And there is additional proof, maestro."

117

Sophie looked quizzically at Holmes, who appeared to relish her attention.

"Examine the areas on each of the instruments where the chin is accustomed to rest as one plays and has consequently worn away the upper layers of varnish. Stradivari primed his violins with a material composed of mineral silicates. It is exceptionally durable, strengthening the fibres of the wood and rendering it waterproof. I suspect that the priming coat is much more responsible for the tone of the violin than the subsequent layers of varnish that are superimposed. As you can see even with the naked eye the substance used for priming the *Medici* is unquestionably different: it is not characteristic of the master's. I speak with some authority, for I have conducted my own investigations on the varnish of stringed instruments, antique and modern, as the Hills will confirm. Here, take my glass."

Del Nero complied and inspected each violin several times with Holmes' lens. He was crestfallen.

"But the sound, Mr Holmes," he muttered tepidly.

"The *Medici* is a superb violin, maestro, there is no question – but it is *not* from Stradivari's hand. All indications point to Jean-Baptiste Vuillaume, an outstanding luthier in his own right, and of course a famous copyist, who knew Paganini well."

Del Nero fell back into his chair, smitten and enervated. I refilled his tumbler.

"Your fiancée, maestro, has a fine mind, a very fine mind, and she doubtless was struck by the incongruities of Father Grancevola's sentimental and all-too-beautiful tale, not to mention the curious conditions he imposed. I am certain you will discover that there is no Father Grancevola in Treviso."

"I have checked, Mr Holmes, and you are correct," said Sophie. "Yes, Helene died there, but that is all I could ascertain. The poor pastor at San Gaetano da Thiene knew nothing about violins, nor of any clergy answering to the name Grancevola, which in the Italian means, as Donato knows, 'spider-crab'."

Holmes stepped across our room to retrieve a large volume, one of many he filled with accumulated scraps and items of interest throughout the years. Leafing quickly through the section under the letter 'M' he withdrew a clipping from *The Times* of London.

"Is this the man who approached you in Venice," he asked, handing the slip to the violinist, "tall, rounded shoulders, a prominent curving forehead with sunken eyes? I believe you said he spoke to you about the motions of heavenly bodies."

The newspaper article described the publication of a brilliant new work on asteroids, and it was accompanied by a sketched portrait of its author: Professor Moriarty. Del Nero stood haggard and agape. I was no less amazed.

"Yes, that is he," the musician whispered. "That face has been imprinted upon my senses and I would recognise it anywhere."

"Here is our spider-crab," declared Holmes triumphantly, "a man for whom the sheer theatrical joy of deception was an intoxicating liquor, and whose reach has extended even beyond death."

"You see, maestro," resumed Holmes, "your Sophie had detected signs of a growing and unnatural obsession that raised its head shortly after your betrothal, an obsession with proving your powers and fearing their loss, so unlike the *homo novus* who had remade himself. Her suspicions about the provenance of the violin to which you were becoming intemperately attached demanded that she inspect it for herself. She took the opportunity that felicitously arose but her plans went 'agley', as the poet Burns might say. She may have wished to prevent the concert from occurring at all, given your increasingly unstable condition. But as I have often told Watson, the psychology of women defies comprehension. What is certain, however, is that she is no Antonia Bianchi, maestro, but rather a Helene von Dobeneck in her devotion to you. Her crime was a crime of love."

Del Nero, after the rigours of his inimitable concert and the strains of the tumultuous denouement of the evening, may be forgiven if all he could manage was to burst into tears and mutely accept the tender caresses of his lover.

Holmes beckoned silently to me and we slipped away out of our rooms to allow the couple a moment of privacy for their rapprochement. My companion had fortunately smuggled a brace of cigars, whose taste and aroma we relished mightily. Moments later an enchanting and ethereal interplay of violin and voice broke delicately upon Baker Street and beyond, drawing our gaze to the firmament above.

"Holmes," I asked softly, and with unabashed reverence, "would you mind very much if I borrowed your copy of the *Odyssey*?"

The Queen's Hall circa 1896

Notes & Selected Bibliography

This section is intended for those readers whose curiosity has been piqued by various elements of the novel, particularly when fact and fiction are suspected to have diverged, and when historical and biographical information may be desired *after* the novel has been perused. The selected bibliography that follows is merely a starting point for further investigations.

Baring-Gould's magisterially comprehensive and highly entertaining *The Annotated Sherlock Holmes*, and the *Grove Dictionary of Music and Musicians* (now *Grove Music Online*) have been invaluable general resources.

Chapter One: *A Dangerous Ennui*

The death of Moriarty had left a vacuum: Professor James Moriarty, brilliant mathematician and criminal mastermind, whose pervasive influence in London was exposed by Holmes. He and the detective met and clashed at the Reichenbach Falls in Switzerland, where 'the Napoleon of crime' plunged to his death (see *The Final Problem* and *The Adventure of the Empty House*).

the Stradivarius he had so felicitously acquired some years before: In *The Adventure of the Cardboard Box* Holmes describes how he came to purchase his fiddle, apparently sometime before 1889, when the adventure is presumed to have occurred (see Baring-Gould, Vol. II, p. 193).

he was prey to dangerous indiscretions: In *The Sign of Four* Watson reports that Holmes used intravenous cocaine, and even morphine, to ward off the dull routine of existence without 'mental exaltation'.

Traumdeutung: Die Traumdeutung (The Interpretation of Dreams) by Sigmund Freud, first published in German in late 1899. The book would go on to create a revolution in our understanding of the human psyche, and represents the foundation of psychoanalysis. Freud's introduction of the technique of free association as a means of gaining access to the unconscious mind is one of his great scientific achievements. An apocryphal account of the relationship between Holmes and Freud has unfortunately gained widespread notoriety, no doubt because of certain sensational 'revelations'. In actuality the detective of criminal behaviour and the detective of the mind enjoyed an exemplary epistolary exchange of ideas spanning several decades. Holmes occasionally travelled to Vienna to consult the Professor, and after Freud escaped the Nazi regime and settled in Hampstead, Holmes hosted him at Sussex on at least one occasion. Their voluminous correspondence is now housed in the Sigmund Freud Archives at the Library of Congress in Washington, D.C., and will be made accessible to the public in the year 2050.

While bees and music: After his retirement to Sussex Downs , which seems to have occurred in late 1903, Sherlock Holmes devoted his time to bee-keeping and even wrote a *Practical Handbook of Bee Culture, with Some Observations upon the Segregation of the Queen* (see *The Second Stain* and *His Last Bow*). His enthusiasm for music is evident throughout much of the Canon, as the complete Sherlock Holmes stories by Arthur Conan Doyle are known to enthusiasts.

I have an interest in the motets of Lassus: In *The Adventure of the Bruce-Partington Plans* Holmes had already begun a monograph on the polyphonic motets of Orlande de Lassus (1532-1594), who along with Palestrina was one of the most influential composers of the late Renaissance.

You know of course the reputation of Antonio Stradivari and his legacy: The definitive biography of the great luthier remains that of the Hill brothers: *Antonio Stradivari – His Life and Work*, published in 1902. Tony Faber's *Stradivarius: Five Violins, One Cello and a Genius* (2004) is a captivating modern account. Holmes' keen interest in violin-making is evident in *A Study in Scarlet*, wherein he instructs Watson about the differences between Stradivarius and Amati violins.

Genius is the province of the male: The Women's Movement was in its infancy, and it was commonly assumed by the male-dominated scientific establishment that women were intellectually inferior to men.

The Authoress of the Odyssey: by Samuel Butler. Butler (1835-1902) was a novelist (*Erewhon, The Way of All Flesh*) and thinker whose wide-ranging mind addressed itself to studies of evolutionary science, art and literary criticism. *The Authoress of the Odyssey*, published in 1897, is a fascinating work of literary detection that makes a very plausible case for female authorship of the Odyssey of Homer. The first adumbration of his theories appeared in 1892 in the *Athenaeum*.

I made the author's acquaintance during my sojourn through Italy after the incident at Reichenbach: After his encounter with Professor Moriarty at the Reichenbach Falls in Switzerland, where he was thought to have died, Holmes travelled widely. This period, known to Holmes aficionados as the Great Hiatus, occurs between 1891 and 1894. In *The Adventure of the Empty House* he recounts having fled to Florence after Reichenbach, where he is most likely to have met Dr Butler returning from his Sicilian researches into Homer's epic.

I've never known you to take much of an interest in literature: Only recently has Holmes' great contribution to Shakespearean scholarship come to light, with the discovery of an unpublished manuscript by Watson dating from the late 1930s: *Sherlock Holmes and the Mystery of Hamlet*.

Public acclaim means nothing to me: Holmes refused a knighthood, as recounted in *The Adventure of the Three Garridebs*.

the story of the Trojan horse first appears in the Odyssey: True, in books four and eight, though the most popular version occurs in Virgil's *Aeneid*.

quandoque bonus dormitat Homerus: 'Even great Homer nods', a Latin proverb from Horace, indicating that the mighty have their lapses.

his work on the binomial theorem and the dynamics of asteroids: See *The Final Problem* and *The Valley of Fear* for Professor Moriarty's scientific accomplishments, and also Baring-Gould's *The Annotated Sherlock Holmes*, vol. I, pp. 82-83.

Wilhelm or Franz Josef?: Wilhelm II (1859-1941), last German Emperor and King of Prussia, ruling from 1888-1918; Franz Josef I (1830-1916), Emperor of Austria and King of Bohemia, reigning from 1848-1916.

Paganini: Nicolò Paganini (1782-1840) is justly celebrated as a phenomenal and ground-breaking virtuoso of the violin, whose compositions and technical innovations revolutionised the use of the instrument. The fantastic nature of his full life nearly defies description. Born in Genoa to a working-class family, he soon achieved notoriety for his musical talents – as well as his gambling and womanising. He became an internationally-renowned – and very wealthy – touring violinist, who cultivated the dramatic and the sensational both in his playing and behaviour. He died in Nice, survived by his son Achille, and the many fine instruments he had collected as a dealer, including of course, those by Stradivari and Guarneri. Paganini's *Twenty-four Capricci for violin alone* (op. 1) are his lasting contribution to the musical literature of the violin. The definitive biography by de Courcy – *Paganini: The Genoese* (1957) – is highly recommended, as are more compact studies by Kendall (1982) and Sugden (1980).

the Queen's Hall: Built in 1893 in Langham Place, Queen's Hall was a popular venue for classical concerts, home to both the Royal Philharmonic Society and the Promenade Concerts. Designed by Thomas Edward Knightley, it could seat up to 3,000 and was renowned for superb acoustics. An incendiary bomb dropped by the Germans in 1941 destroyed it.

the Beethoven concerto: Beethoven's *Violin Concerto in D Major*, op. 61 is a staple of the solo violin repertoire and deemed its crowning glory. It had its premiere in Vienna in 1806.

Joachim, Ysaÿe, Sarasate, Kubelík, Hall, perhaps even young Kreisler: A who's who of great violinists at the turn of the 20th century. **Joseph Joachim** (1831-1907) played the Beethoven concerto at the age of twelve in London, under the baton of Felix Mendelssohn, whose own famous concerto he was among the first to perform, and went on to become one of the most influential violinists in history. He was an early follower of Liszt, from whom he parted ways, however, and a friend of Clara Schumann and Brahms. A superb chamber musician, he founded the Joachim Quartett and also conducted and composed. **Eugène Ysaÿe** (1858-1931) attended the conservatory at Liège in Belgium and studied with Wieniawski and later Vieuxtemps. The 'king of the violin' enjoyed an illustrious solo career: Debussy,

Franck, Saint-Saens and Chausson dedicated their compositions to him, as he united in his playing wonderful technical facility with deep musicianship. Teaching, conducting and composing became more prominent as his bow control and physical maladies worsened, though at the relatively advanced age of seventy he married a pupil over forty years younger. He died in his homeland suffering from morbid obesity, heart failure and the complications of diabetes. The Spanish-born **Pablo de Sarasate** (1844-1908) was known for his prodigious technique and pleasingly flamboyant compositions for the violin. The 'ideal salon virtuoso', he left a legacy that has profoundly influenced succeeding violinists, with his emphasis on precision, consistency and pyrotechnic colour. In *The Red-Headed League* Holmes invites Dr Watson to join him in hearing Sarasate perform at St. James's Hall. **Jan Kubelík** (1880 – 1940) was born near Prague, and before he reached twenty was being hailed as a second Paganini. He first appeared in London in 1900 and was awarded the London Philharmonic Society's Gold Medal in 1902 (succeeding Ysaÿe). As a student he is said to have practiced until his fingers bled. Though he astonished his audiences by an incredible technical virtuosity, his success was relatively short-lived owing to an ostensible lack of intrinsic musicianship. By his thirties his powers had suffered a noticeable decline. The famous conductor Rafael Kubelík was his son. **Marie Hall** (1884-1956), the daughter of an English harpist, studied at the Royal College of Music in London and later, at Jan Kubelík's suggestion, with Otakar Ševčík in Prague. She charmed London audiences at her English debut in 1903. At the Queen's Hall in 1921 she gave the first performance of Ralph Vaughn Williams' *The Lark Ascending*, which was dedicated to her. The Viennese **Fritz Kreisler** (1875-1962) was a prodigy who first studied at the Vienna Conservatory, where Anton Bruckner could be counted among his teachers, and then at the Paris Conservatoire, which he

128

left at the age of twelve with honours. His career was desultory – for a while he attended medical school and served in the army – until 1899 when he won great acclaim with Arthur Nikisch and the Berlin Philharmonic. His playing is marked by tremendous charm and suavity. He composed elegant and graceful salon pieces that are an indispensable part of virtually every violinist's repertoire, his own recordings of which are inimitable. In 1935 a scandal erupted over his musical 'forgeries'. For years Kreisler had been playing certain works by baroque and classical composers, e.g., Pugnani, Francoeur, Stamitz, Vivaldi, Porpora, Dittersdorf and Couperin, which he claimed to have discovered in a convent in France. These were in reality his own compositions.

marriage is not half so bad as you imagine. My Mary was a balm to me: An account of Watson's meeting with and engagement to Miss Mary Morstan may be found in *The Sign of Four*, in which Holmes avers "I should never marry myself, lest I bias my judgment". By 1901 Watson is rooming once again with Mr Holmes, presumably a widower. The actual number of Watson's marriages is a matter of conjecture: according to Baring-Gould he was married thrice.

a group of instruments commissioned by Grand Duke Cosimo de' Medici in the late 17th century: Stradivari made a concerto of instruments for Cosimo III de' Medici, the first of which were delivered in 1690. Three are known to have survived: a viola and violoncello, both relatively large, and the *Tuscan* violin, beautifully described in a monograph by W. E. Hill and Sons. The *Medici* is based upon the unknown violin that disappeared, along with the other viola, from the Pitti Palace after Cosimo's death.

The master's imprimatur: The most authoritative account of Stradivari's labels – and the forgeries and alterations thereof – can be found in the Hills' biography. Watson's

129

transcriptions are accurate, though not absolutely perfect in the most minute aspects of orthography, which could not be expected on the spur of the moment. (I owe thanks to Dr Huma Amer for replicating the labels by hand from facsimiles).

universal modifications essential for the modern player: The development of music for the violin from the 19th century onward, which demanded increasing dexterity and greater tonal range, led to alterations of the original instruments that are now ubiquitous. These include a lengthening of the neck and a flattening of the fingerboard, replacement and reinforcement of the bass-bar and adjustments of bridge and soundpost. The resonating 'box' or body of the violin, however, is generally kept intact and unchanged unless damaged.

I have since had it appraised by Messrs. Hill themselves, our greatest authorities: Following the tradition of their father William Ebsworth Hill (1817-1895), William Henry (1857-1929), Arthur Frederick (1860-1939) and Alfred Ebsworth (1862-1940) became the foremost makers and dealers of violins in England. Their life of Stradivari and their monographs on numerous violins are classics. By 1915 W. E. Hill and Sons of New Bond Street, London, were designated 'Sole Violin and Bow-Makers to His Majesty the King'. In 1901 they would certainly have known of Holmes' instrument, as he would have sought them out not only for confirmation of its provenance, but also for the necessary adjustments to its bridge in the years since he acquired it, and the purchasing of strings. Their common interest in Stradivari goes without saying.

valuable though it was, he treated it with seasoned familiarity: I have Helene Pohl of the New Zealand String Quartet to thank for pointing out that accomplished fiddlers, unlike reverential and nervous amateurs, generally tend to handle their priceless instruments without undue 'preciousness'.

the handiworks of, for example, Vuillaume or Stainer: Two great luthiers. **Jean-Baptiste Vuillaume** (1798-1875) was a renowned French violin-maker and dealer through whose hands passed many of the great instruments of the Cremonese masters. He repaired Paganini's 1742 Guarnerius (the *Cannon*) – albeit under the watchful gaze of the fretful virtuoso – and meticulously reproduced copies of Stradivari's violins, including the famous *Messiah*, which he owned and kept in pristine condition until his death. **Jacob Stainer** (1617-1683) was an Austrian luthier whose violins were characterised by a sweetness of tone and were widely admired – Bach himself possessed one and treasured it. The predilection for a different sound would eventually lead to their eclipse by Stradivari and others. Accused of heresy by the Catholic church, Stainer died in poverty in Absam (the Austrian Tyrol), but for over a century after his death his violins were highly valued and much copied.

Chapter Two: *The Emperor Has No Violin*

I was speechless: Watson's susceptibility to the charms of women is evident throughout the Canon, in contrast to his companion's apparent disinterest. In *The Sign of Four* Holmes, upon hearing of Watson's engagement to Mary Morstan, exclaims: "But love is an emotional thing, and whatever is emotional is opposed to that true, cold reason which I place above all things". In *The Greek Interpreter* Watson writes explicitly of Holmes' ostensible aversion to women.

His violin has been stolen: Sadly, a number of magnificent violins have actually been purloined, never to reappear. They include Louis Spohr's Guarnerius, and the 1732 *Hercules*

Stradivarius taken from Eugène Ysaÿe's dressing room at the Maryinski Theatre in St. Petersburg. The 1713 *Gibson* Stradivarius, belonging to the Polish virtuoso Bronislaw Huberman was stolen twice, first in 1919 and then, in 1936 from Carnegie Hall. Miraculously enough, the *Gibson* was ultimately rediscovered in 1987 when the disreputable fiddler and miscreant Julian Altman confessed on his deathbed to have purchased it from the Carnegie Hall thief (*A Stolen Stradivarius, a 51-Year Old Secret* by Richard L. Madden, *New York Times*, 14th May 1987).

a piano with so fine a temperament as the Erard: The Langham Hotel did indeed house a very fine Erard grand piano, which was tuned not in accordance with 'equal temperament' tuning, but differently – in a way that would have allowed a greater distinction between key signatures, and a more natural accommodation of the harmonies of a stringed instrument. For a fascinating and delightful discussion of the topic of tempered tuning, see Ross Duffin's *How Equal Temperament Ruined Harmony (and Why You Should Care)* (2007). Erard was originally a French firm, founded in 1780, that moved to London and enjoyed considerable success for their superb pianofortes.

The reassuring touch of a physician: Watson was, of course, a physician, having taken his doctorate of medicine from the University of London in 1878. The debate that has ensued about his abilities may be attributed in large measure to misunderstandings deriving from *The Adventure of the Dying Detective.*

the flask of brandy: A medicinal staple throughout the Canon in keeping with the times. In *The Adventure of Wisteria Lodge*, for example, Holmes himself advises Watson to offer Mr Scott Eccles a brandy and soda to allay his nerves.

The police will be an unnecessary interference: The police then, as now, were not relied upon for cleverness or tact, and it is certain that their presence at the Langham Hotel would have caused great consternation and needless alarm among the clientele and staff.

of course I knew of your great reputation even on the Continent: How could she not? As early as 1887 'Europe was ringing with his name' (*The Adventure of the Reigate Squire*).

We strode across the commodious lobby to a wide staircase: See Steel's wonderfully illustrated history of the Langham (1990). The first storey housed the principal suites of apartments engaged by the most illustrious clientele, including royalty. Around it on the outside ran a series of balconies and a supporting ledge that encircled the entire building. When the palatial Langham opened its doors in 1865 it was London's largest hotel.

On the third count I rose and slapped the maestro hard across his cheek: Nowhere in Breuer and Freud's seminal opus, *Studies on Hysteria*, published in 1895 in German, nor in the earlier publications of the French neurologist Jean-Martin Charcot (1825-1893), has any such treatment been advocated. It is likely that Watson derived his knowledge from other sources, most probably British.

and an oilskin: Additional protection for the Channel crossing.

gather your strength while I proceed to Miss Delumeau's suite: As Signor del Nero and Sophie Delumeau were not yet married, it would have been unacceptable to the Langham Hotel establishment for them to have shared a room. When the composer Antonín Dvořák attempted to economise by engaging a double-room for himself and his adult daughter, the hotel manager refused (Steel, p. 46).

It is well-known that at the Langham another element make their home – gamblers, confidence-men and the like:

133

Sinister occultist and charlatan Aleister Crowley, fraudster Horatio Bottomley, and other such figures were regular visitors. A secret cockfighting pit was kept in the basement of the hotel despite the illegality of the activity.

Chapter Three: *Artistic Licence*

His left shoulder seemed slightly higher than his right: A long-standing adaptation, as for Paganini, of physiognomy to the requirements of decades of violin-playing.

I see you hold strong views on one of the most pleasurable of human activities: Del Nero's views on tobacco, unlike those of Holmes or indeed of the medical establishment itself, were far in advance of the times. Though intensely pleasurable, and therefore highly addictive, tobacco has proved to be one of the most significant of all contributors to human illness. Sigmund Freud continued to smoke cigars even *after* he had developed malignancies of the mouth and jaw that necessitated over 30 painful operations. However, both Holmes and Watson, for reasons unknown, appear to have escaped the more deleterious physical effects of an addiction to nicotine every bit as powerful as Freud's.

Joachim, who hoards his Stradivarii: Joseph Joachim owned at least eight of the master's instruments!

I can take the cheapest fiddle of the lowliest student and surpass them!: Fritz Kreisler is said on one occasion to have fooled listeners by surreptitiously substituting an inexpensive trade fiddle for his Stradivarius.

Messrs. Hill would be honoured to lend you one of their own: W. E. Hill and Sons of New Bond Street, in close proximity to the Langham Hotel, would undoubtedly have had a number of superb instruments on hand and would eagerly have lent one to an artist of del Nero's rank.

He peered through the sound-holes: Stradivari's label would have been visible through the sound-hole closest to the G-string.

Ah, a bow of John Dodd – excellent, Mr Holmes, second only to Tourte: The importance of the violin bow was generally underestimated before the 19th century. François Tourte (1747-1835) revolutionised the making of bows by readjusting weight, determining ideal length and calibrating the optimal diameter of the stick. He discovered the superior merits of Pernambuco wood and was renowned for his meticulous workmanship, producing bows that have been unsurpassed. John Dodd (1782 – 1839), known as the 'English Tourte', was born in Surrey and died at the age of eighty-seven in an asylum. His finest bows are considered to be excellent, though his output was not consistent. Dominique Peccatte (1810-1864), initially a luthier, was apprenticed to Vuillaume before setting out on his own. His best bows are considered the only ones genuinely to rival those of Tourte. Del Nero's curious compliment was probably a courtesy, as he would have been far more likely to praise Peccatte. The Hills of London also produced superior bows.

the ridiculous custom of Spohr's: Louis Spohr (1784-1869), a contemporary of Paganini's and a friend of Beethoven's, was a fine violinist, conductor and prolific composer. He is credited with the invention of the violin chin-rest, employed by all performers today with the exception of a small number of baroque and folk artists. His *Violin-Schule* (1832) was one of the most popular violin methods of the time. Is a chin-rest necessary? Paganini, that greatest of all technicians, had no need of one. In my own experiments with the violin, which I approached as an absolute neophyte in preparation for the composition of this tale, I managed without one. Skilled violinists to whom I entrusted my 'naked' instrument seemed

135

to play upon it with customary ease. Insofar as the chin-rest diminishes and alters the contact between the violinist and his/her instrument, it may be considered to be an interference. Video clips of the legendary jazz violinist Stuff Smith show that the chin-rest served ornamental rather than functional purposes. Certainly neither del Nero nor Holmes had any use for the device!

"tis enough, 'twill serve": Mercutio in Shakespeare's *Romeo and Juliet*, Act III, Scene I, after he had been wounded by Tybalt: "No, 'tis not so deep as a well, nor so wide as a church-door; but 'tis enough, 'twill serve". Del Nero is obviously well-read.

that so-called 'violinist to the Queen': Wilma Neruda (1839-1911) was a celebrated Moravian violinist. She was first married to the Swedish musician, Ludwig Norman and after his death she married the pianist and conductor Charles Hallè, who was subsequently knighted, making her Lady Hallè. The title of violinist to Queen Alexandra was bestowed upon her in 1901. She played a 1709 Stradivarius purchased for her by the Duke of Edinburgh and the Earls of Dudley and Hardwicke. In *A Study in Scarlet* Holmes expresses an eagerness to hear her in concert: 'Her attack and bowing are splendid' he says. Sir Charles, incidentally, was spellbound by Paganini, whom he visited while in Paris in 1838.

My accompanist mistook it at first for my Medici, but he is a Russian and is only just returning to music after a mental collapse: The great Russian composer, conductor and pianist Sergei Rachmaninov (1873-1943), after the premiere of his First Symphony in St. Petersburg in 1897, did indeed suffer a collapse and nearly forsook music altogether. For Rachmaninov's own account of the incident, his treatment with hypno-therapist Nikolai Dahl, and his re-emergence with the composition of his Second Piano Concerto, see Riesemann (1934). He made his London debut as a pianist at Queen's Hall in April 1899. It would have been technically (but not fictionally) impossible for him to have accompanied del Nero on 27th October 1901, as this was the very same day he premiered his Second Concerto – a much less daring work than the First Symphony – to considerable acclaim in Moscow.

the Hoffmann Barcarolle: The Barcarolle from Offenbach's *Tales of Hoffmann* had served Holmes quite well in *The Adventure of the Mazarin Stone.*

When you practice, devote some time to playing very slowly and very softly: Del Nero's recommendation to practice slowly and softly would have won the approval of Leopold Auer, one of the great pedagogues of the instrument. It would ultimately be taken to heart by Holmes in his later years in Sussex, as my discovery of Watson's lost manuscript on the mystery of *Hamlet* illustrates (Garcia, 2008).

In the early morning I perform my Swedish exercises: As did the characters of P. G. Wodehouse, and the humourist himself (though perhaps not always in the morning).

Musicians are athletes, Mr Holmes: Without a doubt, a fact that is far too often overlooked. The rate of physical injury among musicians is extremely high, and education in the maintenance of physical well-being requires consistent emphasis.

Chapter Four: *A Demoiselle in Distress*

For this relief, good Dr Watson, much thanks: Miss Delumeau is also familiar with Shakespeare – in this case, *Hamlet*, Act I, Scene I.

the Baroness Helene von Dobeneck: Miss Delumeau's account of Helene von Dobeneck née Feuerbach (1808-1888) is correct in every factual detail, including the depth of her love for Paganini. Matters touching upon the *Medici* are of course imaginary. In a letter to his friend and adviser Luigi Germi on 30 August 1830, Paganini wrote: 'It would be far more fitting if I should marry another. This is the daughter of a famous (or rather *the* most famous) writer on jurisprudence in Germany (M. de Feuerbach), a knight of many orders, the intimate counselor of the King of Bavaria, and president of the city of Ansbach. His daughter, whose name is Helene, is a baroness, having married a baron three years ago – but not for love. She is passionately fond of music and sings extremely well. She came to Nuremberg to hear me and begged her husband to bring her again to my second concert. After having heard, seen, and spoken to me, she fell so much in love with me that she no longer knows any peace of mind and will die if she doesn't eventually get me'. (De Courcy, Vol. I, p. 414). The forty-eight year old violinist would never again be loved so fully by a woman.

the peerless Manuel Garcia: Manuel Garcia (1805-1906), is widely regarded to be the 19th century's greatest vocal teacher, who indeed developed Helene von Dobeneck's 'beautiful and brilliant' instrument (De Courcy, vol. I, p. 417). He also achieved world fame as the inventor of the laryngoscope. He does not, alas, appear to be a relation of the author of *The Case of the Missing Stradivarius.*

the buffoon of the violin who imitated the sounds of animals: It is true that Paganini indulged in such theatrics, and could employ his talents in the service of mimicry, winning over the gallery. When in Ferrara in 1812, however, after he imitated the braying of a donkey in repayment for their hissing of a ballerina whom he had accompanied on guitar, he was run out of town by an enraged populace, unaware that the inhabitants of Ferrara were known as 'donkeys' to their neighbours! No doubt this was one of the anecdotes with which Sherlock Holmes regaled Dr Watson over a bottle of claret in *The Adventure of the Cardboard Box*.

who played trick pieces on a single string: Paganini's popular *Napoleon Sonata* and other works were composed for the G-string alone, from which he elicited marvels.

The public Paganini played a Guarnerius violin: Paganini played a number of violins, but the 1742 *Cannon* was his favourite, famous for its rich and powerful sonority. He obtained the Guarnerius sometime between 1802 and 1804 while in Leghorn, where a wealthy businessman, M. Livron, lent him the instrument. After hearing Paganini play, he surrendered it to the virtuoso on the condition that no one but he would ever be permitted to use it. Paganini kept his promise and upon his death left it to his native Genoa. A decade later in Parma Antonio Pasini, a famous miniature painter and music-lover, challenged Paganini to execute a difficult concerto at sight, offering him a valuable violin if he succeeded. Naturally Paganini met the challenge and won the violin, presumed to be a Stradivarius. In 1818 Paganini purchased a Stradivarius from Count Cozio di Salabue of Casale Montferrato and used it frequently in concert.

he used his scordatura, performed those insipid duets on the G and E strings alone: Scordatura is a term used to imply an other-than-normal tuning of the strings of the violin to produce exceptional effects of colour, range and musical 'atmosphere', of which Paganini was a master. Paganini's *Duetto Amoroso* was composed for a lady at the court of Lucca and depicted a conversation between lovers, using only the top and bottom strings of the violin (G and E).

The theatrical antics described are true, as was his performing among the dead at the cemetery of the Venetian Lido. It is also true that he played the chamber works of the masters in private. There is no evidence that he ever performed any of his greatest compositions, the *Twenty-four Capricci for violin alone* (op.1), in public. A reviewer opined:

'There is only one thing to be desired with regard to Paganini. We should exceedingly like to hear him play an adagio movement of any great master' (Sugden, p. 151).

he left Helene a singular gift: If Paganini did, it is not recorded in his biographies, and it could not have been the *Medici* violin.

rather than sell his birthright for the pottage of virtuosic display: An allusion to the book of *Genesis*, 25, wherein Esau, famished from a day in the field, surrenders his birthright to his cunning brother: 'Then Jacob gave Esau bread and pottage of lentils; and he did eat and drink, and rose up, and went his way. Thus Esau despised *his* birthright'.

the church of Saint Louis en L'Île: The magnificent church on the Île Saint-Louis in Paris, one of two natural islands on the Seine and an historic oasis. Much brighter than the Cathedral of Notre Dame, the church was consecrated in 1726, its construction having begun in 1644; it is a perfect home for musical performances and today concerts are held there throughout the summer months.

by engaging Lestrade's men: The ferret-like Inspector Lestrade of Scotland Yard features in many of the Sherlock Holmes stories. He is tenacious, though conventional and lacking in imagination, but Holmes and he develop a certain mutual respect despite their vast differences of character and approach to criminal detection.

The glove was a signal: Could the literary Watson have been unaware of Romeo's words, 'O, that I were a glove upon that hand, That I might touch that cheek!' (*Romeo and Juliet*, Act II, Scene II)?

Holmes, I am sure, would have deployed his Irregulars: The Baker Street Irregulars were Holmes' juvenile street-wise assistants whose help proved invaluable when clandestine surveillance was essential, as in *The Sign of Four*.

Mr Holmes moves in mysterious ways his wonders to perform: An allusion to *Light Shining Out of Darkness* by the popular English poet and hymnodist William Cowper (1731-1800):

> 'God moves in a mysterious way
> His wonders to perform;
> He plants his footsteps in the sea,
> And rides upon the storm'.

my experiences of the battlefield in Afghanistan: Watson was attached as Assistant Surgeon to the Fifth Northumberland Fusiliers, seeing action in the second Afghan war. Colonel Hayter, who figures in *The Adventure of the Reigate Squire*, was treated by Watson in Afghanistan.

Chapter Five: *The Fate of the Medici*

Damn you, Watson: Strong language for the detective. On one occasion, in a fit of exasperation, he remarked, 'Old woman be damned!' (*A Study in Scarlet*), but he is never known to have addressed his companion thus.

a hundred of the finest – Cuban no less!: Then, as now, Cuban cigars were regarded highly. Two boxes containing fifty cigars each would when bundled lengthwise have approximated the size of an uncased violin.

I idled away at billiards: In *The Adventure of the Dancing Men* we learn that Watson never played billiards without his friend Thurston. This instance may have been the exception, understandable in light of the circumstances.

The astute physician is one who can see beyond a bewildering array of symptoms to divine the illness beneath: The Edinburgh physician Dr Joseph Bell (1837-1911) was the model on which Conan Doyle based his detective. In a letter of 4th May 1892 to Bell, he wrote: 'It is most certainly to you that I owe Sherlock Holmes ... and I do not think that his analytical work is in the least an exaggeration of some effects which I have seen you produce in the out-patient ward' (Baring-Gould, Vol. I, p. 8).

the new Dupin: C. Auguste Dupin is the first fictional detective, created by Edgar Allan Poe in *The Murders in the Rue Morgue,* and a boyhood hero of Conan Doyle's. Sherlock Holmes, however, did not think much of him: 'No doubt you think that you are complimenting me in comparing me to Dupin' he observed. 'Now, in my opinion, Dupin was a very inferior fellow. That trick of his of breaking in on his friends' thoughts with an apropos remark after a quarter of an hour's silence is really very showy and superficial. He had some analytical genius, no doubt; but he was by no means such a phenomenon as Poe appeared to imagine' (*A Study in Scarlet*).

Paganini could not help but play the clown: Indeed, and though Paganini's programmes offered showpieces that emphasised drama and incredible technical virtuosity, great contemporary musicians were transported by his playing e.g. Schubert, Meyerbeer, Schumann, Rossini and even Liszt, who wrote, 'What a man, what a violin, what an artist! God, how much of suffering, misery, torture is in those four strings' (quoted from Wechsberg, p. 237). Paganini *did* love to play Mozart and Beethoven quartets, as the violinist Carl Guhr reports, but never in public (Schonberg, 1988, p. 115). His rival Louis Spohr wrote that Paganini told him his style was calculated for the masses, and when he finally had the occasion to hear him play, remarked, 'In his compositions and his style of interpretation there is a strange mixture of consummate genius, childishness, and lack of taste, so that one is alternately charmed and repelled' (Sugden, p. 60).

In 1684 the Marchese Bartolommeo Ariberti ordered from Antonio Stradivari a group of instruments for the court of the Grand Duke of Tuscany, Cosimo III de' Medici: Completely true. Cosimo III de' Medici (1642-1723) ruled over Tuscany for fifty-three years. Known for his melancholy disposition, and reactionary and anti-semitic laws, his wife Marguerite Louise d'Orléans abandoned him, fleeing to the Convent of Montmartre in France and renouncing her title. Cosimo presided over a precipitous decline of Tuscan power.

In 1794 one of the violins was sold by a Florentine, Signor Mosell: Mosell sold what has come to be known as the *Tuscan* Stradivarius to a Mr David Ker in Ireland for the sum of £25 (Hill, 1976).

as his singular gift to Hector Berlioz attests: Hector Berlioz (1803-1869), the great French composer whose own life reads like a Balzac novel, was approached by Paganini after the latter had acquired a large Stradivarius viola and wished to display its properties. Berlioz composed *Harold in Italy*, a marvellous symphonic work featuring the oft-neglected instrument. It was, alas, not what Paganini had in mind: he felt that he as the violist should be playing the entire time, so he composed his own viola work which, unlike *Harold*, is now seldom performed. Nevertheless, his admiration for Berlioz' genius was profound. Paganini attended a performance of *Harold* conducted by Berlioz on 16th December 1838 in Paris. The composer writes: 'The concert was just over. I was in a profuse perspiration and trembling with exhaustion when Paganini, followed by his son Achilles, came up to me at the orchestra door, gesticulating violently ... Paganini, seizing my arm, and rattling out, "Yes, Yes!" with the little voice he had left, dragged me up on the stage, where there were still a good many of the musicians, knelt down and kissed my hand. I need not describe my stupefaction' (De Courcy, Vol I., pp. 285-6). Shortly thereafter Paganini made a present to Berlioz of 20,000 francs.

Beethoven spento ...: These are the exact words of Paganini's letter to Berlioz of 18th December 1838 (De Courcy, Vol. I, p. 287); the English translation is my own. His magnificent generosity rescued Berlioz, who was seriously in debt, alleviated his burdens and made the composition of his great *Romeo and Juliet* symphony possible. Paganini's gift to the man was a gift to mankind.

It was an allongé Stradivarius: We do not of course know the particulars about this lost violin, but del Nero's description of the measurements of a long-pattern Stradivarius is accurate. Faber (2004, p. 48) notes: 'Long Strads are still beautiful. Their varnish is redder and tougher than on earlier violins, with an almost bottomless depth of colour. Stradivari was at his peak as a craftsman when he made them; and his long pattern pushed the design of the violin further than anything achieved before'.

an Amati: Most probably a violin made by Nicolò Amati (1596-1684), grandson of Andrea, in Cremona, who developed grand-pattern instruments larger than his predecessors'. A 'Grand Amati' is highly prized today. Stradivari may have been apprenticed to his workshop.

Man's reach should always exceed his grasp: An allusion to lines from Robert Browning's poem *Andrea del Sarto* (1855): 'Ah, but a man's reach should exceed his grasp, or what's a heaven for?' Del Sarto – like del Nero – was a Florentine.

I had rendered Bach that evening, the D-minor partita without a break: The *Partita* in D minor for solo violin (BWV 1004) by Johann Sebastian Bach is in five parts, concluding with the monumental *Chaconne*. It is recognised as one of the masterpieces for solo violin, and to be able to execute it without pause is a feat of which few violinists are capable, as playing for any length of time on the instrument necessitates retuning. Temperature, humidity and the tension of playing will create changes in the length of the strings and consequently affect intonation. Such changes must be accommodated spontaneously – and continuously – by the violinist during performance, whilst maintaining concentrated interpretative vigour.

Church of the Madonna dell'Orto: In the Cannaregio area of Venice, this magnificent Gothic church is filled with paintings by Tintoretto. Off the beaten tourist track, it is marvellous haven for the serious listener and musician.

such felicity of tone and timbre as could hardly be imagined despite its years of idleness: An unplayed violin, like an unwatered flower, will eventually wither away. If neglected for long periods of time, its tonal properties can generally be restored only gradually by playing.

San Gaetano da Thiene: One of Treviso's smallest churches, situated in the heart of the city. It dates from the 14th century. There is no evidence of a link between it and Helene von Dobeneck.

preferring instead to turn the troubles of his countenance merely upon himself: Like Brutus in Shakespeare's *Julius Caesar*, Act I, Scene II: 'Cassius, Be not deceived: if I have veil'd my look, I turn the trouble of my countenance Merely upon myself'. Watson's familiarity with the Bard is to be expected.

Chapter Six: *A Portrait of the Violinist as a Young Artist*

this violin of yours – I think it fancies me!: Violinists frequently speak of their instruments as if they are live companions with unique temperaments and character, a consequence of the unparalleled intimacy demanded by their relationship.

chanced to pass a gypsy camp ... My mother and her brothers were playing their fiddles: There is a long and rich tradition of gypsy violin music and players that has run in parallel with classical music, though occasionally the trajectories have intersected. The Hungarian violinist Ede Reményi (1828-1898) was classically trained at the Vienna Conservatory. His playing, infused by gypsy influences, inspired Brahms' *Hungarian Dances*.

chief of my delights was the time we gave to improvising on classical and folk themes: The art of improvisation has virtually no place in the classical music conservatory of today, even though Bach, Handel, Mozart, Beethoven, Chopin, Liszt *et al.* were accomplished improvisers. Jazz and other genres have carried on the tradition of improvisation in the West.

left-handed pizzicato: Pizzicato refers to the plucking of the strings of a bowed instrument with the fingers, generally of the bowing hand. Left-handed pizzicato is a rather difficult manoeuvre.

The true secret of technique, however, is relaxation: Virtually every musician would agree with this, though optimal relaxation is more easily discussed than achieved.

my colleagues had often been beaten and coerced into developing their talents: Coercion has been a mainstay of musical pedagogy over the centuries and even today has a prominent role. Paganini, who was first taught by his father, writes: 'If I did not appear to be working sufficiently hard, he would force me to make more effort through starvation. I suffered a great deal physically ... but there was no need for him to be so severe' (Kendall, p. 9). Del Nero and Yehudi Menuhin are examples of great virtuosi who were spared the rod.

including Prague, where Paganini himself had failed: In Prague during the summer of 1828 Paganini was severely criticised; audiences were relatively sparse, and his pyrotechnical feats did not impress a population desirous of more depth. Del Nero's triumph in that same city must have been a source of immense satisfaction.

my life was a life of ceaseless travel: Not least of the challenges of the successful musician are those posed by the practical and artistic travails associated with touring.

the Mendelssohn and Beethoven concerti: The Violin Concerto in E minor (op. 64) by Felix Mendelssohn, premiered in 1845, is one of the most important, popular and frequently performed violin concerti and is considered a litmus test for any aspiring virtuoso. The Beethoven concerto, as mentioned previously, is acknowledged to be the most profound, though as in all things musical, *de gustibus non est disputandum.*

Like my famous countryman I found myself in a dark wood where the right way had been obscured: An allusion to his fellow Florentine Dante Alighieri, and the opening lines of the *Divine Comedy* (Inferno, Canto 1):

*'Nel mezzo del cammin di nostra vita
mi ritrovai per una selva oscura
che la diritta via era smarrita'.*

"Là ci darem la mano, Vorrei e non vorrei": From Mozart's opera *Don Giovanni* (K 457), with libretto by Lorenzo da Ponte. Near the end of Act 1, Don Giovanni attempts to seduce the newly-married Zerlina: '"Let's entwine our hands," he urges, "I would like to, and I wouldn't like to" she replies'.

"Greater than that," added Sophie, "since you must include variations of phrasing.": Advantage, Miss Delumeau.

savage Russia, where an extraordinary new music is emerging: Del Nero is probably referring to the innovations begun by the so-called 'mighty handful' – Moussorgsky, Rimsky-Korsakov, Cui, Balakirev and Borodin, a group of self-taught musicians who had begun to compose music of striking originality with a distinctly national flavour. He would also have been acquainted with the Tchaikovsky *Violin Concerto in D Major* (op. 35), but we do not, alas, know his sentiments about this piece, now a concert staple.

Chapter Seven: *The Science of the Stradivarii*

William E. Hill and Sons, Violin-Makers: The premiere violin-making establishment of England, at 140, New Bond Street, W., renowned both for their biographies of luthiers and also particularly for their bows, thanks to the efforts of Alfred Hill, who trained in Mirecourt, the famous French centre for violin-making. Arthur was a collector and historian, and Wiliam Henry, the senior member of the firm, played viola. Many great Cremonese violins passed through their hands. Their illustrated monographs on the *Tuscan* and the *Messie* first published in 1891 are superb.

Its pianissimo carries to the furthest reaches of a hall with a fullness that is without equal: The hallmark of a great instrument. As Peterlongo (1973, p.95) notes: 'The present writer has more than once witnessed the enthusiasm of distinguished performers for a modern instrument which sounded superb in the restricted space of a workshop. Great was their disappointment when they heard the same instrument in a large hall ...'.

you and your brothers are nearing completion of your biography of Antonio Stradivari: It was published in 1902. The elaborate first edition, meant for wealthy collectors, sold out its run of a thousand copies in only three years. In 1909 a less expensive edition was produced, which proved to be even more popular. It is an extraordinarily comprehensive and well-written work, providing a wealth of knowledge about Stradivari's life and working methods.

Your contribution to our chapter on Cremonese varnish: The detective was of course one of the pioneers of forensic chemistry, and the recipient of a posthumous Honorary Fellowship from the Royal Chemistry Society. However, it appears that he did not apprise the Hills of his most important discoveries concerning Cremonese varnish, namely, the presence of *propolis*, a substance created by bees for use as a sealant in their hives, and the composition of the priming layer used to treat the outer surfaces of the violin's body before the application of varnish proper.

the king of instruments: The 'gender' of the violin is a matter of debate. In Italian and French it is a masculine noun, while in German it is feminine. Its shape may be considered 'ambisexual', making it both King and Queen together.

Only pine, by which I mean of course *Abies pectinata* or *Picea excelsa:* Abies pectinata (silver fir) and Picea excelsa (spruce fir) are both members of the Pine family.

Stradivari's formula for varnish: The exact formula is still a mystery, but even more mysterious is its specific influence on the sound of the violin. Arguments about the role of varnish are innumerable and baffling, and attempts at exact compositional analyses have been inconclusive. The Hills' (1976 p. 179) opinion is representative of the majority: 'Fine varnish will not compensate for bad material or faulty construction; but that it makes or mars the perfectly formed instrument is, in our opinion, beyond dispute'. Others, however, take more extreme views. Nagyvary (see *Nature* **444**, 565 (30 November 2006) and www.nagyvaryviolins.com) credits the varnish used by Stradivari and his peers – rather than their craftsmanship – with responsibility for the superiority of their instruments, while Beament (*The Violin Explained*, 1997) dismisses it altogether.

Stradivari's great-great-grandson Giacomo ...: The facts related here are correct, except that he never divulged the actual formula to anyone – neither his relatives nor the Hills. As Signor Giacomo Stradivari wrote in a letter quoted by the Hills (1976, p. 168) to one Signor Mandelli: '... the Bible, inside the cover of which was written, in the handwriting of Antonio Stradivari, the famous recipe for the varnish and how to apply it, was destroyed. Previously, however, I made a faithful copy of the same, which I have jealously guarded, and which I have never been willing to part with, notwithstanding the repeated solicitations of M. Vuillaume and others'.

'Is it not strange that sheeps' guts should hale souls out of men's bodies?': From *Much Ado About Nothing*, Act II, Scene III. Violin strings were then made out of the intestines of sheep (*not* cats!). Though metal and synthetic strings have come to dominate today, the sound of a bowed gut string is marvellously rich and distinctive. String-making is itself a highly complex craft.

Antonio Stradivari lived into his nineties, and he died a very rich man in Cremona: True. He survived two wives and fathered eleven children, dying at the age of ninety-four. In Cremona 'rich as a Stradivari' became proverbial.

That, you fool, is the secret of his violins!: As good an explanation as any perhaps. There is no record of the real Arthur Hill having advocated a demonic theory, however, nor of behaving diabolically.

he kissed the handle of the stick, murmuring, "A prince among bows.": He was apparently kissing the 'frog' of the violin bow.

Paganini, Ysaÿe, Joachim, Sarasate, del Nero, and Holmes himself: Eccentric all, Paganini even more so, since he cultivated his reputation as the 'Devil's Fiddler', which was only enhanced, for example, by rumours that he had learnt his craft while in prison for having murdered an unfaithful mistress.

this invention, so simple in its magnificence, of using a bow upon a gut string, changed humankind: Bowing upon a string is a relatively recent human invention, dating back only hundreds, rather than thousands, of years. See James Beament's *The Violin Explained* (1997) for a precise and fascinating description of pitch, tone, timbre and harmonics as they apply to the sounds produced by a bowed violin.

Except the human voice: Miss Delumeau has a point. For a discussion of the role of the voice in the evolution of multiple steady-pitched sounds (probably insignificant) see Beament's *How We Hear Music* (2001, pp. 148-9), which is also strongly recommended for its elucidation of the acoustical foundations of music.

Helmholtz and Fourier: Hermann von Helmholtz (1821-1894) was a renowned German scientist whose treatise *On the Sensations of Tone* (1863) is considered to be the seminal contribution to the science of acoustics and music. Helmholtz discovered 'that a pitched musical sound is made up of a number of pure tone components called its harmonics. The process is called harmonic analysis. It is also called Fourier analysis, because some forty years earlier the French mathematician Fourier had shown theoretically that any complex vibration could be so analysed into component harmonics' (Beament, 2001, p. 33). Miss Delumeau's discussion of fundamentals and harmonics ('overtones') is scientifically accurate. In fact, she has corrected and amplified the great man's theories.

rem acu tetigisti: A Latin proverb meaning, literally, 'you've touched the thing with a needle'. 'You've hit the nail on the head' is a more idiomatic, but less delicate, English equivalent.

Chapter Eight: *Intermezzo*

a new age of criminal detection: Holmes has undoubtedly been influenced by Professor Freud's work on dreams.

the passionate but cowardly attitude of the Latin male towards the weaker sex: From the English perspective, which in all probability would be disputed by the inhabitants of France, Spain or Italy.

mens sana in corpore sano: The Latin proverb meaning 'a sound mind in a sound body' derived from the poet Juvenal.

a particularly challenging scene from a relatively new Italian opera: Giacomo Puccini's *Tosca*, which opened in Rome in 1900, is one of the most beloved and popular of operas today. Miss Delumeau's electrifying performances in the title role of Floria Tosca are credited with having resuscitated the opera's fortunes after its disappointing premiere.

as Holmes strutted and fretted: It would soon be his hour upon the stage ...

Chapter Nine: *The Food of Love*

all of musical London – and many from continental Europe – were in attendance: At Ysaÿe's performance of Elgar's Violin Concerto in Berlin in 1912, the greatest violinists of the day were present, including Kreisler, Elman, Flesch and Marteau.

he plays only with the middle section of the bow: Fritz Kreisler was rather unique in playing thus.

the Czech – no, the youth with that great mane of hair: Jan Kubelík, who was even younger than Kreisler.

the Belgian – Ysaÿe! He has grown as wide as his vibrato!: Ysaÿe would have been at the height of his powers. He pioneered the use of vibrato for the violin and to members of the older tradition of playing e.g. Joachim, it would have seemed foreign and excessive. In 1912 his technique began to plummet, which some attributed to a faulty grip of the bow. There is incidentally no record of Holmes' use of vibrato, but we may justifiably surmise that it was minimal.

Joseph Joachim: The great Hungarian master whose bowing technique was marked by a highly angled wrist.

the Spaniard is a trickster: Sarasate did indeed have such a reputation, and Holmes' anecdote about his stage trick is true. He also dyed his moustache.

Corno di Bassetto has returned from the grave: The pen-name of a famous writer whose musical criticism in London during the years 1890-94 was legendary. Here is a small but characteristic sample, from 1893: 'Last Monday week I heard them give a tremendous ovation to Joachim, who had played Bach's Chaconne in D minor, and played it, certainly, with a fineness of tone and a perfect dignity of style and fitness of phrasing that can fairly be described as magnificent. If the intonation had only had the exquisite natural justice of Sarasate's, instead of the austerity of that peculiar scale which may be called the Joachim mode, and which is tempered according to Joachim's temperament and not according to that of the sunny South, I should have confidently said to my neighbour that this particular performance could never be surpassed by mortal violinist'.

The audience is politely requested to refrain from applause: A most unusual request but one in keeping with del Nero's ideals.

His hands were immense and his face marked by an indescribable sadness: Sergei Rachmaninov, only just emerging from the aftermath of a crisis occasioned by the premiere of his First Symphony in 1897. He was dogged by melancholy through much of his life.

the virtuoso's homage to the monarch we still mourned: Queen Victoria died on 22nd January 1901, her reign of over sixty-three years being the longest of any British monarch's.

Schubert's waltz: From Soirées de Vienne, valse caprice for piano No. 6 (after Schubert D. 969 & 779) S. 427/6, by Franz Liszt. Del Nero is playing his own arrangement for violin of a piano composition by Liszt based on waltz themes in Schubert's *Valses Nobles* and *Valses Sentimentales*. The Russian violinist David Oistrakh is known to have performed the *Valse Caprice* in recital.

Del Nero non ripete!: A variation of 'Paganini non ripete', an idiomatic Italian saying derived from an instance when Paganini adamantly refused to give an encore.

that breath upon a bank of violets of which our dearest Shakespeare wrote.: Twelfth Night, Act I, Scene I:

If music be the food of love, play on;
Give me excess of it, that, surfeiting,
The appetite may sicken, and so die.
That strain again! it had a dying fall:
O, it came o'er my ear like the sweet sound,
That breathes upon a bank of violets,
Stealing and giving odour!

Chapter Ten: *Voilà*

the drunken Glazunov was wholly to blame: Alexander Glazunov (1865-1936), Russian composer and conductor. He is rumoured to have been inebriated during the premiere of Rachmaninov's First Symphony in St. Petersburg, which he conducted. Rachmaninov fled after hearing the performance and nearly renounced composition altogether (see Garcia, 2004).

An old pseudonym, Watson: For the Irish playwright, novelist, journalist, critic, socialist and vegetarian George Bernard Shaw (1856-1950). His musical criticism, collected in *Music in London: 1890-1894* is delightfully intelligent, provocative, penetrating, and immensely readable. Shaw was awarded the Nobel Prize in 1925 and is the author of over sixty plays.

eletricismo: Paganini used this very term, which implied a palpably charged electric force.

Antonia Bianchi: When Paganini met this attractive twenty-year old singer in 1824 he was twice as old as she and suffering from maladies that aged him beyond his years. She soon bore him his only child, Achille, but much to Paganini's dismay her voice was of far more interest to her than motherhood. They lived and toured together for several years, though unmarried. He complained bitterly about Bianchi's incessant jealousy and temper, which led her to smash at least one violin and even to box his ears in public. They parted in 1828, Paganini having settled a large sum upon her while keeping custody of his beloved son. The violinist, no angel when it came to women, had apparently met his match.

A correspondent of mine in Vienna would find a rich symbolism in your choice: Professor Freud of course, but exactly how he would have interpreted the symbolism is unclear as he was generally opposed to assuming universal meanings.

listening with a third ear, if I may coin a phrase: Listening with the Third Ear is the title of a popular book by Viennese psychoanalyst Theodor Reik (1888-1969), published in 1948, which described the psychoanalyst's use of unconscious intuition. Reik, who was Freud's student, must have been all ears when his teacher lectured on the parallels between the methods advocated by Holmes and his own at a meeting of the Vienna Psychoanalytic Society in the 1920s.

a 'wolf' tone: A disagreeable sound often produced by the cello, but also occasionally on the violin, caused by the resonance irregularities of an instrument's structure.

In 1729 for reasons unknown the great luthier began to employ the Roman 'v' for his surname on the labels. Before that it invariably appeared in what is a semi-cursive form, resembling a 'u': True, with one apparent exception – a violin of 1727. There is *no question whatsoever* about the labels of his earlier violins: the 'v' form is not present. (See Hill *et al.*, 1963, p. 218.)

Stradivari primed his violins with a material composed of mineral silicates ...: Many years later the renowned violin-maker and restorer S. F. Sacconi (1895-1973) would identify potassium silicate ('waterglass') as the substance employed by

Stradivari for his priming coat, which is believed now to be far more important than the subsequent layers of the varnish proper that were superimposed, and from which the primer was insulated (see Peterlongo, pp. 59-62, for one of the clearest discussions of this vexing topic, as well as Nagyvary, 2005). Sacconi, who examined and repaired hundreds of Stradivarius violins, revealed his discoveries in *I Segreti di Stradivari* (1972). It is not surprising that Holmes would have anticipated Sacconi, given his formidable powers of chemical analysis (*Holmes, Chemistry and the Royal Institution* (1998) by Richards and Gore).

All indications point to Jean-Baptiste Vuillaume, an outstanding luthier in his own right – and of course a famous copyist, who knew Paganini well: Vuillaume made many superb copies of Stradivari violins, which included a facsimile label that would invariably be dated '1717'. He did not attempt to pass his copies off as originals (though he once briefly fooled Paganini with a replica), but this would not have deterred others, once having acquired them, from doing so. Vuillaume's instruments, however, *sound* different, a fact that is attributed partly to the differences between his and Stradivari's varnishes. How Vuillaume came into possession of the *Messiah* Stradivarius is the stuff of legend. Upon the death in 1855 of Luigi Tarisio, a carpenter of humble birth who acquired and dealt in violins to the point of obsession, Vuillaume hurried to his ignorant heirs and purchased on the spot an immense cache of valuable instruments, among them the *Messiah* and a score of other Stradivarii (see Hill, [*Le Messie*] 1976, and Faber, 2004).

homo novus: Latin for 'new man'.

her plans went 'agley', as the poet Burns might say: From *To a Mouse* by the great Scottish poet Robert Burns (1759-1796):

'The best-laid schemes o' mice an' men
Gang aft agley,
An'lea'e us nought but grief an' pain,
For promis'd joy!'.

the psychology of women defies comprehension: In *The Adventure of the Second Stain* Holmes exclaims: 'And yet the motives of women are so inscrutable ... How can you build on such a quicksand? Their most trivial action may mean volumes, or their most extraordinary conduct may depend upon a hairpin or a curling-tong'.

Selected Bibliography

Auer, L. (1980). *Violin Playing As I Teach It.* Dover Publications, Inc.: New York.

Baring-Gould, W. S. (1967). *The Annotated Sherlock Holmes (Two Volumes). The Four Novels and the Fifty-Six Short Stories Complete by Sir Arthur Conan Doyle.* Clarkson N. Potter, Inc.: New York.

Beament, J. (1997). *The Violin Explained: Components, Mechanism and Sound.* Oxford University Press: London.

Beament, J. (2001). *How We Hear Music: The Relationship Between Music and the Hearing Mechanism.* The Boydell Press: Woodbridge.

Boyden, D. (1965). *The History of Violin Playing From Its Origins to 1761.* Oxford University Press: London.

Butler, S. (1967). *The Authoress of the Odyssey.* University of Chicago Press: Chicago & London. (reprint of original edition published in 1897 in London).

De Courcy, G. I. C. (1957). *Paganini: The Genoese.* 2 volumes. University of Oklahoma Press: Norman.

Duffin, R. W. (2007). *How Equal Temperament Ruined Harmony (and Why You Should Care).* W. W. Norton & Company: New York and London.

Faber, T. (2004). *Stradivarius: One Cello, Five Violins and a Genius.* Macmillan: London.

Garcia, E. E. (2004). Rachmaninoff's Emotional Collapse and Recovery: The First Symphony and Its Aftermath. *Psychoanalytic Review,* **91**, 221-238.

Garcia, E. E. (2006). A Practical Program for Enhancing Technique in Players of Stringed Instruments. *American String Teacher,* February 2006, pp. 50-52.

Garcia, E. E. (2008). *Sherlock Holmes and the Mystery of Hamlet.* In Garcia, E. E., Jaynes, R. and Maguire, E. (2008) *Sherlock Holmes and the Three Poisoned Pawns.* Irregular Special Press: Cambridge.

Grove Music Online.

Hill, W. H., Hill, A. F., & Hill, A. E. (1963). *Antonio Stradivari: His Life and Work (1644-1737).* Dover Publications, Inc.: New York. (Reissue of book first published in 1902).

Hill, W. E. & Sons. (1976). *The Tuscan and Le Messie.* W. E. Hill & Sons: London.

Kendall, A. (1982). *Paganini: A Biography.* Chappell and Company/Elm Tree Books: London.

Nagyvary, J. (2005). Investigating the Secrets of the Stradivarius. *Education in Chemistry,* July 2005, pp. 96-98.

Nagyvary, J. *et al.* (2006). Wood used by Stradivari and Guarneri. *Nature,* **444,** 565.

Peterlongo, P. (1979). *The Violin: Its Physical and Acoustical Principles.* Paul Elek: London.

Richards, A. J. and Gore, B. (1998). *Holmes, Chemistry and the Royal Institution.* The Irregular Special Press: Cambridge.

Riesemann, O. von (1934). *Rachmaninoff's Recollections Told to Oscar von Riesemann.* Macmillan: London.

Sacconi, S. F. (1972). *I Segreti di Stradivari.* Libreria del Convegno: Cremona.

Schonberg, H. C. (1988). *The Virtuosi.* Vintage Books: New York.

Shaw, B. (1949). *Music in London 1890-94,* 3 Volumes. Constable and Company: London.

Steel, T. (1990). *The Langham: A History.* Hilton Press: London.

Sugden, J. (1980). *Niccolo Paganini: Supreme Violinist or Devil's Fiddler?* Midas Books: Tunbridge Wells.

Wechsberg, J. (1972). *The Glory of the Violin.* The Viking Press: New York.

CPSIA information can be obtained at www.ICGtesting.com
Printed in the USA
235729LV00002B/146/P